THE ADVENTURES OF

J.W. Santee

J.W. WALLACE

Fulton Books, Inc.
Meadville, PA

Published by Fulton Books 2022

ISBN 978-1-63860-978-0 (paperback)
ISBN 978-1-63860-979-7 (digital)

Printed in the United States of America

CHAPTER 1

The Meeting: Red Hair and Long Legs

Friday morning

As J.W. came out of the auto parts store, he sees the sky is gray with possible rain. He thinks to himself, *Well, I don't think I will be able to put this new supercharger kit on my SSR[1] today.*

He popped the tunnel cover and dropped the tailgate down so he can get the kit in his truck. As J.W. shut the tailgate, he saw a lady trying to catch her little dog. As the dog ran by, J.W. scooped it up. It was one of those hairless Taco Bell dogs. Not his type. But *she* was!

As she walked over, she was wearing a well-fitting dress, the kind that wrapped around her. It was green, and it made her red

---

[1]   An SSR is a truck that Chevy put out from 2001 to 2006. It's a truck version of a Corvette it sold new for $50,000.

hair really stand out. She was about five feet eight tall in the six-inch stilettos she had on. Her legs were long and shapely.

As she got closer, she looked at J.W. and smiled—not a "Thanks for catching my dog" smile but the kind you get from someone who wants to get to know you. As she was just about to go to him, she tripped in one of the potholes. He reached out and caught her just before she went down. As he lifted her up, she grabbed his arm. As he made her stand up, the little dog started to bark. To his surprise, J.W. had forgotten he had the little guy in his right hand with her in his left.

She took the dog from him and said, "You must think I'm a clod. I can't hang on to my dog or walk." She gave him a sheepish smile.

He asked, "Are you okay? How is your ankle?" He dropped the tailgate.

J.W. lifted her and sat her gently on the tailgate. She looked a little bewildered. He asked if he can see her ankle. She crossed her legs, the hurt ankle on top.

J.W. looked for damage. He thought, *What a lady*, and that she had the nicest legs he had seen in a long time. He said, "It looks a little swollen. Maybe you should stay off it for a little while and put ice on it."

As she looked at it, she said, "I was just about to go get some dinner when he [the dog] ran off. Would you care to join us?"

J.W. said, "I have nowhere else to be right now. I would love to, but under two conditions: one, I drive, and two, I pay."

She smiled a cheerful smile and said, "It's a deal."

J.W. asked, "Do you need anything from your car?"

She said, "Just the kennel in the back seat."

J.W. opened the passenger door to the SSR. He picked her up and gently sat her in the seat. The little dog licked his face. She let out a giggle He retrieved the kennel and locked her car up for her, putting the kennel in the bed. He flipped down the tonneau cover and flipped up the tailgate.

As he walked around to the driver's door, he could hear the little dog yapping. J.W. climbed in and handed the woman her keys. "You might need these."

She rolled her eyes.

J.W. asked, "Do you like steak?"

She replied, "Yes, I do."

He took her to a place he liked. "It ain't real fancy, but they make a great steak."

As they arrived, J.W. parked and walked around to open her door. He put his hand out to help her out of the truck. They walked toward the door. She took his arm. He felt a little squeeze of his arm muscle.

She said, "No wonder you could just lift me like nothing."

He thought, *Not bad for a guy about to turn fifty.*

They walked in. The little dog was in her purse, and they were about to sit down. J.W. held the lady's chair for her. She looked surprised as she sat down.

He asked, "What would you like to drink?" He sat down across her.

She said, "Whatever you're having."

He ordered two shots of Tarantula tequila and two George Killian's beers, his favorite.

"So what do you do?" she asked.

J.W. said he was an ex-rodeo rough stock rider and US Army Ranger, but now he works for the US postal service. He works on the machinery.

"And you?" he asked.

She looked confused. "I don't do anything. My family is big in oil."

"I see. So why are you here with me?"

"Because you're the first real man I have ever met. You know nothing of me but helped me, anyway. You're not after my money or what my family can do for you because you didn't know about them. So why did you help me?"

"Because." J.W. laughed a little. "I will help anyone in need. I was raised that way."

She said, "And you have manners."

"I know it's a lost art these days, but I like them. Plus, if I didn't, my mom would tan my backside, so I use them. It's just part of who I am."

Her smile became bigger, with a glint in her eyes. About that time, the drinks arrived. She held up the shot glass. "To manners."

He toasted with her. Then they ordered their steaks. They talked throughout dinner.

J.W. thought, "She is a very down-to-earth girl with the body of an angel."

The dog fell asleep as they talked. When dinner was done, they walked out the door. She took his arm again, but she snuggled up to him as they reached the truck. He unlocked the truck and opened the door. He offered his hand to help her in.

As he shut the door, he felt someone behind him. He stepped to his left as he turned. A man tried to hit him with something. He flew past J.W. Then J.W. reached out to grab his collar. J.W. pulled hard on the back of the man's coat, pulling the man off the ground as J.W. slammed him on the parking lot.

J.W. put a knee on the back of the man's neck. Then J.W pulled out his gun and put it against the back of the man's head. The man came to, and he started to move. J.W. pushed the barrel of the gun into the back of his head, and the man stopped moving.

J.W. asked, "Why are you trying to hurt me?"

The man said he was only here for the lady.

"Well, the lady is fine. You're the one in trouble here."

As the man turned his head to look at J.W., J.W. could see the man had a broken nose. J.W. patted him down and found two guns and a wallet. J.W. removed all three.

J.W. said, "I'm going to let you up. You move in any way, I will shoot you."

Understanding, the man said, "Yes, sir!"

J.W. stood up and backed up.

She opened the door and stepped out of the truck. "Are you okay?"

J.W. said, "I'm fine. He's the one bleeding." He spoke to the man. "Okay, you can get up now."

The man stood up. He turned slowly.

J.W. thought, *Guess he took my warning seriously. Good for him.*

As he looked at the lady, the man said, "Miss Ginny, are you all right?" The man asked J.W., "Can I reach into my pocket?"

"Okay, but slow."

The man pulled out a red handkerchief so he could stop the bleeding from his nose.

J.W. asked Miss Ginny, "Do you know this guy?"

She looked embarrassed. "Yes, he works for my father."

The bleeding man said, "You missed your security check-in." The man was sent out to find her.

J.W. said, "Well, she's fine and very safe, as you can see."

The young man said to Miss Ginny, "Please call your father. We found your car, and knowing you, your father got worried."

J.W. handed the man back his wallet. J.W. emptied the guns and cleared them before he let the man have them back. J.W. had all six clips.

He said, "When she gets home, you may have these back." Then told the man to go get cleaned up. "We will be here calling her father."

The man said, "Okay." He went inside the steakhouse.

She reached for her phone. "It is dead. Can I use yours?"

J.W. handed her his phone. Miss Ginny punched in the numbers, and she began to explain things to her father.

The young man came back.

J.W. said, "You check out. Here's your clips. Are you okay?"

The young man said, "I'm a little embarrassed, and my pride is hurt, but I will be okay. You're pretty fast for an old guy!"

J.W. smiled and said he had military training.

The young man said, "Oh, I see. That explains a lot. My name is Richard. And you?"

J.W. said, "J.W. Santee."

The man put his hand out. J.W. took it.

"Nice to meet you," Richard said.

About that time, Miss Ginny came over. "I'm so sorry about all of this. I don't even know your name."

"It's J.W., Miss Ginny."

Richard said, "Mr. Santee was kind enough to forgive me, Miss Ginny."

CHAPTER 2

The Unexpected Visitor

Friday night

"Well, that was nice of him," Miss Ginny said.

Richard told her, "But your father would like to meet Mr. Santee."

She said, "Well, he will have to wait. After all, we just met, and we are not through with our evening."

Richard said, "Yes, but your father—"

J.W. said, "The lady said not now, and I'm not inclined to jump at his beckoning. He has a rude way of asking."

She said, "Pick up my car, please. I won't be needing it tonight."

The man looked like she had just kicked his dog. But there was nothing he could do. He walked over to J.W. with his hand out. "It was nice to meet you. I'm sorry for my rudeness."

J.W. took his hand; the man had a firm grip. J.W. liked this young man. He just didn't know why yet.

J.W. said, "If you use manners, you will get a lot further in life."

Richard said, "I will keep that in mind." Then he turned and walked away.

She jingled her keys at Richard. He turned, came back for the keys. As he held his hand out, she placed them in his palm.

She looked at him. "Don't worry, Mr. Santee and I won't say a thing about what happened here. Besides, I like you."

Richard blushed a little bit. "Thank you, Miss Ginny."

As he turned and walked away, she turned to J.W. and said, "Well, that was exciting. You have anything else for me tonight?"

"Well, it's not real exciting, but it's fun. Let's go out to the Hall of Fame bar and do a little two-stepping."

She looked puzzled. "I don't know how to two-step."

J.W. said, "Well, it's time you learned. You live in Tulsa, Oklahoma. You need to know how to two-step."

She smiled. "Okay, let's go."

"Well, you're going to need a different pair of shoes. It's going to be really hard in six-inch stilettos."

She said, "Let's drop by my place. I have a set of boots I think you will like."

J.W. said, "Okay, where to?"

As he held open the door, she took his hand to sit in the truck. When J.W. closed the door, he thought, *What have you gotten yourself into?*

As he got in, she gave J.W. directions to her place. They pulled up.

J.W. asked, "Which condo is yours?"

She giggled. "It's not a condo complex. It's all one house."

J.W. just whistled. "This is all yours? What do you do with all this space?"

She just smiled. "It's not that big."

"Okay, if you say so."

J.W. put the truck in park. He hopped out to get her door. As she swung her legs out, her dress came open at the knee. He put his hand out for her as he turned his head. J.W. could feel the warmth of her hand in his as she stood. She stepped out of the doorway and took J.W.'s arm. She squeezed his bicep again. Now he wanted to giggle but didn't.

J.W. shut the door and walked with Miss Ginny on his arm. They reached the steps leading to her front door. The door was about twelve feet tall and eight feet wide, made of solid oak. She saw him looking at the door. "It's kind of heavy."

J.W. said, "I would think so."

It must have weighed eight hundred pounds. She handed him the key. He unlocked the door and pushed hard. It flew in easily. It almost pulled him off his feet, but he braced his leg and stopped it before it hit the wall. He looked a little embarrassed. It opened easier than he thought, sorry.

She was on the verge of laughter but held her composure. As he held the door open, she walked past. He shut the door much easier this time. He could feel the lock click into place. As they walked into the main room, he just stood there, looking around.

J.W. said, "This room... This is bigger than my whole house and shop together!"

About that time, a young lady in her twenties came in. She greeted Miss Ginny. As the two ladies talked, he looked at the architecture in the room. It was very nice. Just because he couldn't afford something like this doesn't mean he couldn't appreciate it.

The young lady walked over, as two other women came into the room. J.W. didn't even see them come in. They went down a long hallway. The first lady came to J.W. and asked if he would like to have something to drink. He had no idea what he was supposed to say. "Maybe a beer?"

She could see J.W. was nervous, and she asked, "What kind?"

He smiled. "I like Killian."

She looked at him and said, "Just a moment sir." She walked away.

J.W. was a little taken back. It's been a long time since anyone called him *sir*. So here he was in a room big enough to play football all by himself. The term *out of his element* was an understatement.

Soon, the lady came back with the beer. It was a Killian's. He was surprised.

He thought, *Now if I just had a shot of Tarantula tequila, I just might feel a little more at home here in the echo chamber.*

As he drank his beer, Miss Ginny came in wearing a silk shirt and denim skirt and the fanciest boots he had ever seen. She was a cowboy's dream. As he finished his beer, she walked over to him.

Miss Ginny said, "Will this do?"

As he picked up his jaw off the floor, he said, "Well, you're going to turn a few heads." He was thinking everyone's. She looked finer than a 98 score on an eight-second buck out. She had it together.

"Do I need anything?"

J.W. said, "Just your ID. That's a state requirement."

She looked into her purse. She pulled out her ID and a key and handed them to J.W. He put them in his right button-down pocket.

The first lady came back and collected his beer bottle. Miss Ginny handed her the purse and said, "My car should be returning."

The lady said, "It's in the garage, ma'am."

Miss Ginny said thank you. She then turned to J.W. "Is there anything else, sir?"

He looked at Miss Ginny and then back at her associate "I didn't get your name," he said to the associate.

Now she looked shocked. "It's Michelle."

"Well, Miss Michelle, you serve up a very cold beer. Thank you."

Michelle looked a little flushed. J.W. thought he may have embarrassed her.

Miss Ginny looked at her and said, "Isn't he just the nicest guy? And a gentleman too."

Michelle said, "Yes, ma'am, very nice."

J.W. looked at her and said, "It was very nice to meet you. Good night now."

As he and Miss Ginny turned for the door, he opened it much easily this time. As she stepped through, he closed the huge door. She took his arm, and they walked down the stairs to his truck. He opened the door and helped her in. As he closed the door and went around the truck, he saw two men in black suits standing by an SUV, also black.

J.W. thought, *Why do they wear black suits and drive black SUVs? Is it a rule somewhere?*

He got in his truck, and he told her they had company. She looked confused.

"Two guys in black suits and a black SUV."

Miss Ginny rolled her eyes. "My dad."

He figured as much. "Well, hold on. Got your seat belt on?"

She said, "Yes, why?"

He put the SSR in reverse. He hit the gas, went straight back to the SUV. When he was about twenty feet from it, he turned the wheel hard to the right as the front of the truck slid. He dropped it in the drive. By the time the two guys figured out what he was doing, J.W. and Miss Ginny were out of the gates and on their way down the hill.

His SSR can take these corners faster than any SUV, and they were gone. They hit I-44 east to 193rd Street. At the end of the off-ramp, most of the traffic was going to the Cherokee casino to the left. They went right at the light and right into the quick trip. He asked if she wouldn't mind waiting, he had to get some cash. So she waited in the truck.

As he got out, he had a thought. So J.W. walked back to the back of his truck and looked under it. That was what he thought. There was a little black box attached to the bottom of the truck bed. He popped it off and went inside. As he came out, he put the black box in the bed of a Ford as it drove away.

Well, that takes care of that, he thought.

He got in the truck. She asked what he was doing at the back of his truck. He said he was just checking something. As they pulled out of the parking lot, they went right. The old Ford went back up on I-44. They went about fifty yards and turned in. They were there, at the Hall of Fame. They parked. He escorted her to the door. He paid the fee at the door.

They went inside. She had never been inside a honky-tonk before. It was like she was in a whole new world. He took her hand and led her to the dance floor. The floor was about thirty feet across and fifty-five feet long, with a band at the far end and on a stage about chest high. He showed her the basics, and they were off. They danced all night. She turned some heads.

At the end of the night, he took her home. When J.W. pulled up, the guys in the SUV did not look happy. He parked the truck. Got out to open her door and helped her out. They walked up the stairs to her front door. She was a little wobbly as he pulled the key and her ID out of his pocket.

She smiled and asked if he wanted to come in for the night. He opened the door and handed her a key and her ID.

He said, "That would not be proper as you're intoxicated. I will not take advantage of you in this situation."

About that time, Michelle came to the door. Miss Ginny looked at him and asked him if he was sure. He didn't want to stay.

"Not tonight, but thank you for the invite."

Then Michelle took Miss Ginny inside.

"Good night," Michelle said, as they closed the door.

He walked down the stairs to his truck, where the two guys from the SUV were standing. About the time J.W. got to the bottom step, Richard walked out the door.

Richard said, "You two gentlemen, one of you do this." Richard hands him a piece of paper. To the other man, he said, "You're dismissed."

Richard turned to J.W. with his hand out. J.W. shook hands with Richard. The two men walked away, grumbling.

Richard said, "They didn't need hurt. They're still young. How are you?"

J.W. said, "I'm fine."

"Where did you learn to drive like that?"

"Escort duty."

Richard said, "Well, there's quite a lot to learn about you, Mr. Santee."

J.W. said, "Good night, Richard."

He replied, "Good night, sir."

J.W. handed him one of his cards. "If Miss Ginny wants to know how to get a hold of me, here's my card. That will get you some points in, maybe. Thank you."

J.W. got in his truck and went home.

What a night. What a wonderful night, he thought to himself.

C H A P T E R   3

Security Breach

Saturday morning

As J.W. awoke the next morning, he wondered if it was all a dream. But by the way his legs were feeling, he knew it was real.

He got up and grabbed a shower. He was not sure about all this hair. He normally keeps his hair in a high and tight flattop, but a month ago, his best friend—Mike Pantuso—and he made a pact to grow their hair for the kids with cancer so the kids can have hair. He used a blow-dryer to dry it straight back. It's brown now. When he was growing up, it was platinum blond, but time and age change everything. There's gray mixed in now.

He shaved but kept the Fu Manchu mustache; he had grown accustomed to it. He got dressed in his old faded jeans, a brushpopper shirt with no sleeves, and cowboy boots. He went to the kitchen to have breakfast. He had six rolled tacos with cheese and guacamole with a big glass of milk.

My kind of breakfast, he thought.

He went out to the shop. J.W. was going to put the E-Force supercharger on this morning. When he turned off the alarm system and went inside, J.W. could see that things had been moved. He went upstairs and unlocked the office. It had a high-tech lock and code system on it. A close friend of his, David Tudor, designs home alarm systems for the big boys and manufacturers and tests them there. He had a camera system that worked independently from the alarm.

J.W. watched a black SUV pull into the drive and around back to the gate. They got out and messed with the alarm system. Once inside, they looked around for what J.W. didn't know. Then they came upstairs and tried to get into the office but seemed to have no luck there.

Good job, David.

David will have to improve the design on the system that the men got past.

And then the men left.

So J.W. went down, unlocked the big door, and opened it up to find a man standing there. J.W. moved to a defensive stance; he realized it was Richard.

"Well, good morning, Mr. Santee. Miss Ginny would like you to meet her for dinner at her house at 7 p.m."

J.W. said, "Richard, don't you get tired of doing all the running around for her? And it's J.W., not Mr. Santee. He was my grandfather. I'm just a plain everyday guy, so just call me J.W. Okay?"

Richard looked surprised. "Sure thing, Mr.—I mean, J.W. Yes, sometimes, but the pay is really good."

J.W. thought about that. "Well, you can't argue with that. As long as you're happy."

Richard said, "About dinner?"

J.W. looked at him for a moment. "Please tell Miss Ginny I would love to have dinner with her."

Richard asked, "Miss Ginny did have a question. What she would like to know, what was the brand of tequila you two shared?"

"Oh, that was Tarantula tequila. The blue one."

"Thank you again."

J.W. said, "Before you go, tell your men if they step foot on my property again we will have a discussion they won't like. I found some things moved in my shop this morning, and I have them on CD."

Richard looked surprised. The men were not authorized. "I will take care of this, J.W."

"See to it. I'm not as nice as they think I am."

Richard turned and left.

J.W. watched him as he walked out of the driveway. He respectfully parked on the street.

J.W. liked that in this man. Mutual respect.

He got to work on his SSR, first removing the hood then disconnecting the battery. He removed the fuel rails and the intake bolts after removing the throttle body. He lifted the intake manifold out and pulled all the injectors. He was ready to put the new system together.

After he installed everything, he had to go back to the workbench to get the second part to this system: a 200 horsepower nitrous oxide system.

J.W. put the new sprayer plate behind the throttle body; they linked up perfectly. He tightened everything up, reconnected the battery.

Well, now we find out.

He turned the key. It fired right up and sounded great. There was a new whine to the motor. He would have to get used to it in time. He then mounted the NOS bottle in the bed of the truck and ran the lines. All done. What time is it? It's 5:30 p.m.

Great, he had time to grab a shower and go to dinner. He pulled out his black long coat and a bolo, with an Indian dancer on it, in turquoise coral jet and other stones. It was his father's. Big Jim had made it himself back in the seventies, and J.W. had always liked it.

He looked into the long mirror. He thought, *I guess I looked okay*, with his black cowboy hat and Western long coat, blue jeans, and boots. He had a pink shirt on with the bolo from his dad. He was off to dinner.

J.W. pulled up, and Richard was there to greet him. "These two men have something to say to you."

The men walked up. Both apologized for messing with his shop.

"It won't happen again," one said.

He said, "I would hope not." He slid back his long coat around the sides of his body, revealing his shoulder holster with his .45-70[2] revolver sitting in it.

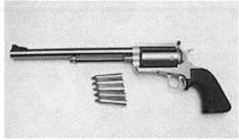

Richard's eyes got slightly bigger.

J.W. said, "Thank you, gentlemen. I would like for us all to be friends."

They turned and left. It was just him and Richard now.

As they watched the two men, Richard turned to J.W. and asked, "Do you have a concealed weapons license?"

"Yes, I do. Thank you for asking."

"Good," Richard said. "What is that? That's not what you used on me."

J.W. said, "No, this is my .45-70 revolver from BFR. I had my Hi-Point 380 the other day. I change guns as much as I change what I'm driving or riding, depending on what I'm doing."

J.W. gave Richard a spare bullet from the right side of the holster. The bullet was about the size of an average index finger.

Richard said, "You shoot these!"

J.W. smiled. "Not if I don't have to. That's three dollars a pop. Well, I better get up to the house for dinner."

As they walked, J.W. said, "I can tell you wanted to ask me something. Okay, what's up?"

Richard looked uneasy. "I have to ask you for your weapons, J.W. It's policy here."

"Okay," J.W. said. "But we will do it inside, okay?"

Richard said, "Sure, that would be fine."

As they walked inside, they saw Michelle was there. She asked J.W. if she could take his hat and coat.

J.W. looked at Richard. "You knew she was in here, didn't you?"

---

2 The BFR .45-70 is a very large handgun; it holds rifle rounds. An old military rifle round, it's a car killer.

Richard smiled as J.W. took off his coat. Her eyes got big, and then J.W. took off the shoulder rig and handed it to Richard, who walked over to a curtain, pulled it back to reveal a small door. He unlocked it, set the gun inside, locked the door again, and then pulled the curtain back.

Michelle was still standing. "Your hat."

"Oh, I'm sorry." J.W. removed his hat.

She hung the hat on pegs in a small room. The pegs were spaced far apart—for cowboy hats, J.W. guessed. As Michelle showed him into the dining room, J.W. felt small.

This house is huge.

She told him where to sit and that Miss Ginny should be here soon, and she walked out a side door.

Then a young man came through another door. With a small cart, he came up to J.W. and asked what kind of beverage he would like. About that time, Michelle came back into the room with a George Killian beer and a shot of Tarantula tequila. She told the young man that J.W. preferred that, and she was right.

The tequila was cold, just like J.W. liked it. So was the beer. He drank the shot and sipped the beer.

As everyone left, it was so quiet he could hear his own heartbeat.

Then Miss Ginny came in. She asked, "Did we get the right beer and tequila?"

J.W. said, "Perfect, thank you. You look amazing."

She had her hair down—long and flowy, just like he liked. Her dress was light blue, one of those long ball gowns, and a little of it followed behind her on the floor. The front of the dress came up to show her ankles and shoes—so she could walk, he guessed. She also had on a diamond necklace. It all looked too perfect to be real.

As she sat down next to him, she rang a little crystal bell. He didn't even see it. As she set the bell down, six doors opened. People had plates, bowls, and saucers. Others had silverware napkins, and yet, others had champagne glasses and water glasses. It was like a small ballet. They went around the table.

As a younger girl poured water, a middle-aged man—in his thirties, J.W. guessed—poured champagne for Miss Ginny. The man with the cart from earlier brought J.W. another beer and shot. He told the man, "Thank you."

J.W. asked Miss Ginny, "Do you eat like this all the time?"

She giggled. "No, I normally eat out."

About that time, all the doors came open again as they brought out vegetables, mashed potatoes and gravy, and the biggest steak he had ever seen: a rib eye medium rare.

She looked at him. "Medium rare, right?"

"You have a good memory."

She said, "I do try."

The steak was perfect. The mashed potatoes were garlic, his favorite. The vegetables were perfect. He didn't know who cooked all this, but it was the best he ever had.

"Please tell them thank you for me."

She giggled again.

"What is with the giggles?"

She said, "I like watching you eat. You're a good eater, and you smell so nice. What are you wearing? Is that Stetson cologne?"

"Why, yes, it is. How did you know?" He had always worn it. "I always have. Can we leave this room? I feel a little uncomfortable here in such a big room with only two people in it."

She said, "Sure we can. Would you like to take a walk around the grounds?"

"Sure, but in that dress? It would be ruined. Maybe you should change."

"Okay, I'll be right back. Feel free to roam the house."

J.W. thought, *Roam is right. The place is huge. She must have an army to clean it.*

About that time, the man with the cart came. "Would you like another beer, sir?"

"No, thank you. I'm driving, but thanks for the offer."

The man just bowed his head and walked away. About that time, Miss Ginny came back in jeans and Reeboks.

"Now that's more like it." J. W said. She still looked stunning.

She just smiled and took his arm. "Where would you like to go? The pond, the lake, the stables, or the lawns?"

"How big is this place?"

"Two hundred sixty-five acres."

"Just for you?"

She giggled again. "No, the help and their families use it too."

"Why do you have such a big place?"

She had inherited it from her grandparents. Miss Ginny had always loved this place.

"It just seems so big my whole place would fit in the main room of your house," J.W. said.

As they walked, she asked about where he grew up and his family and just general questions like that.

As they got closer to the house, J.W. said, "It's getting late, and I have to work in the morning."

"I thought you said you don't work till three."

"Yes, that's right, but I have work to do around my house."

"Sorry, are you sure I can't talk you into staying the night?"

"Not tonight. That would be improper this soon. Maybe next week."

She gave him a little pouty face. He kissed her long and deep. As he held her in his arms, J.W. never wanted to let her go.

When they stepped apart, he looked at her. "Good night, Miss Ginny. I will be thinking of you."

He turned toward his truck.

As he reached his truck, J.W. thought, *My gun and coat.*

He looked up. Richard was standing there with both. He held the rig so J.W. could slip into it and then his coat as Richard handed him his hat.

Richard said, "I couldn't let you ruin a great good night like that by forgetting your things, so I saved you a trip."

J.W. smiled. "Thank you, Richard. I owe you one."

"I think this makes us even."

J.W. unlocked the truck and got in. "Good night, my friend."

Richard smiled. "Next time you go to shoot that thing, I'd like to go with you."

"You got it, Richard," J.W. said. "I normally go on Wednesdays."

He drove off.

CHAPTER 4

The Black Ferrari

Saturday night

As he reached the main gate, J.W. looked to see if anyone was following him tonight. Nothing so far. He pulled down out of the hills and got on I-44. He had noticed a set of headlights that had been behind him from halfway down the hills. Not that uncommon. There was only one way in and out. He slowed down to see what they would do.

When J.W. slowed, they slowed. He was thinking, *A clear straight road. Why not test the new motor parts?*

So J.W. hit the open switch for the nitrous oxide and put the pedal to the floor. The SSR screamed to life. As he looked back, he saw the car was right behind him. J.W. reached over and hit the nitrous oxide; the truck felt like it was about to take flight.

He looked down at the speedometer; it was off the numbers, and they stop at 140. He just looked straight ahead and felt the g-force hold him in his seat. J.W. looked in the rearview mirror. The lights were way back there. As he crossed the Arkansas River, he turned off the NOS, got in the right lane, took the off-ramp with the lights off, and waited for them to just drive by. It was a black Ferrari.

They couldn't be after me in a Ferrari. Oh well.

It was not his fault they couldn't keep up in that overpriced toy. He waited for about two good songs on the radio: Hank Williams Jr.,

"Whiskey Bent and Hell Bound"; and Garth Brooks, "The Thunder Rolls." Garth lived in Owosso. J.W. had never seen him.

J.W. fired up the truck and went home, watching his rearview. He thought, *I had better lock everything up tonight.*

He put the SSR in the shop and then locked the back gate, just in case. He even locked the doggy door so his ninety-eight-pound boxer couldn't have some fun if anyone comes around. Lord help them, because he wouldn't.

It's getting close to 11:00 p.m. Time for bed. He set the alarms in the shop, the house, and the yard so anything bigger than a hundred pounds would be in for a world of hurt.

J.W. went to bed.

CHAPTER 5

Off in a Jeep

Sunday morning

The next morning, J.W. had to go to work. The weekend was over for him.

It was a beautiful Sunday morning. He drank his coffee on the back porch, with Rocky at his feet asleep and snoring. It was a nice morning.

J.W. saw a face peeking through the back gate. Rocky came off the floor with a bark that startled J.W. He took off at the fence. The person on the other side was on the run.

J.W. ran into the house to look out the front window. He got there just in time to see a black Ferrari pull away.

What the hell is going on here?

He went back to his desk and looked at the footage: they pulled into camera range to a house to the left and stopped across the street. They sat there for a while then got out. It was a tall thin man wearing a white polo shirt and shorts, and with a good tan. He had wavy blond hair.

J.W. got lucky: the man looked right at the camera. He stopped it and printed out the man's pic. J.W. walked up the driveway; on camera 2, he walked to the fence and looked around. J.W. didn't know why. It was an eight-foot gate with sheet metal over it. The only place one can see in was where it lached, and then all one can see was his back porch. They had to squeeze their face between the house and the gate to see in.

Well, I will give this pic to David. He's a good Internet guy. If it's out there, he will find it.

Oh well, back to his coffee.

J.W. drank his coffee, thinking, *What kind of idiot would drive a Ferrari in this neighborhood to spy on me? Hell, they stick out like a pumpkin in a watermelon patch. They must be a real piece of work. It's time to eat.*

He was thinking, *Four eggs over easy, hash browns, deep fat fried, and bacon.*

As he got the eggs going, he cut up four small potatoes—all he had—into really small pieces, covered them in cayenne pepper and garlic, dropped them into the deep fat fryer, and checked on the eggs and bacon on the flat plate. Time to turn the eggs and bacon. Salt and pepper and cayenne pepper. Flip one more time. That's it. Pop the hash browns and the drip bacon on paper towels. Okay, everything was ready.

Got his favorite bowl: a long crystal bowl his mom had given him. It had a flat bottom and low sides. Perfect for this and hot dog cheese.

Got his bowl, put the hash browns on the bottom, four eggs on top, bacon on the edge. He almost forgot: a large glass of Braum's whole milk. Now it was time to eat.

The trick was not to break the yolks until they were on the hash browns. Then cut them up over the hash browns, and "go to town."

J.W. finished. Rocky gave him that look of "Where's mine?" So J.W. gave him two Beggin' strips from his treats bag. He was a sucker for that. Time to clean up.

Then Rocky went nuts. It was that idiot in the Ferrari again. He heard Rocky and floors it.

This was a residential street with lots of kids, so J.W. grabbed his gun. He ran out the door, but the Ferrari was down around the corner.

Damn.

J.W.'s neighbor came out from across the street. "What was that all about?"

J.W. didn't have a clue, but he intended to find out.

The neighbor then saw the gun in J.W.'s hand.

J.W. saw his look. "The guy was looking in my gate this morning."

The neighbor said, "That's odd. I won't even do that, and we are friends!"

J.W. asked him to keep an eye out; he had to go to work soon.

The neighbor said, "Sure. Any trouble, I will call the cops."

J.W. went in and cleaned up and got ready for work: soft-soled shoes and a work shirt. Now he was ready to work for the US postal service. J.W. thought he would take the jeep just in case Mr. Ferrari was watching. The jeep is a 1974 CJ5: no top roll cage, no seat belts, and the windshield still lays down. It got thirty-six-foot boggers on it, so there was no need for a radio. One couldn't hear it, anyway.

On J.W.'s way to work, he didn't see anything. No sign of his new friend.

"Oh well, off to work." He got in the gate and parked. As he jumped out of the jeep, his phone went off. "Hello? Please hold."

"Hi, J.W., how was your morning?"

J.W. asked, "Who is this?"

"It's Miss Ginny."

J.W. said, "Oh, sorry about that, you sound different on the phone. It was okay. Some clown came to my house this morning in a black Ferrari and was looking through my fence."

She said, "Really? Whatever for?"

J.W. said, "I don't know, but I will find out. I have to get in to work. Is this your home number?"

Miss Ginny said, "Why, yes."

"Do you have a cell phone?"

"Yes."

J.W. said, "Text me both your numbers, please, so I can call you when I get off work. Maybe we can go out."

"Okay, I will take care of that."

"Thank you. Goodbye." J.W. rushed in to get on the clock.

A friend asked, "Is the SSR okay?"

J.W. said, "Yeah, it's just a nice night to ride in an open-top jeep!"

Well, the night wasn't too bad, pulled a jam. *Why do people put pens in envelopes and mail them? They can't go through the machinery.*

He spent half his night pulling things out of the pulleys on the equipment. Then a few belts needed to be replaced, and a few gates. Typical stuff. Well, that was over, so he called Miss Ginny. "So what are you doing?"

She said, "Just waiting for your call."

J.W. said, "Yeah, right. I'm not that important to anybody to wait for my call."

"Oh, really? Well, I was waiting."

"Well, I feel important now." He felt like a horse's ass. "So would you like to go out somewhere tonight?"

Miss Ginny asked, "On a Sunday night?"

"Sure. There's plenty to do. This is Tulsa."

"What do you have in mind?"

"Let me meet you at my favorite bar, the Harvard."

She said, "Okay. What do I need to wear?"

"Just jeans, shoes, and a shirt. Nothing fancy. It's 11:40 now, midnight soon. They close at 2 a.m."

"Okay."

27

He got into the jeep and headed to the Harvard bar. When he got there, the crowd was humming from the football games all day and the great songs. The jukebox was playing. Amber was behind the bar, and Nikki was making the rounds. They were a good team and *hot* is an understatement. They were both good-looking.

J.W. walked in. Nikki saw him first and gave him a big hug. "So how was work?"

J.W. said, "Same old sh———t."

He looked over. Amber had his beer and shot in her hands. He held one finger up. He went to the end of the bar. He stopped, and Amber handed him both. He did the shot, handed her the glass, then got a hug. They had been doing this for a long time. It's good when your bartender knows what you like and has it ready for you when you get to her. The shot? You guessed it, Tarantula tequila and a Killian's beer.

Sometimes it's good to be me, J.W. thought.

He talked to a few friends, just general BS. Everyone started staring at the front door.

J.W. said, "Is there a fight?"

It was Miss Ginny in painted-on capri pants, sneakers, and a low-cut T-shirt. J.W. saw her look around; she saw him. J.W. walked over to meet her. He met her. She took his arm. They walked back to where he was standing. The guy sitting next to him got out of his chair and offered it to Miss Ginny. As J.W. thanked him, Miss Ginny sat down. He couldn't stop looking at her. She was so beautiful.

She noticed and asked if something was wrong.

J.W. said, "With you, nothing. You're gorgeous just the way you are."

She smiled in a loving way. As they talked, he looked around the room. He looked from one face to another, and the men were envious of J.W. And the ladies? Well, he didn't have a clue what they were thinking"

She said, "You're always looking around."

"Sorry. It's a habit I got in the military, and it has served me well. Same as sitting with my back to the wall."

"And you can handle yourself."

J.W. said he does okay.

A good song came on the jukebox. J.W. asked, "Would you like to dance?"

Miss Ginny asked, "Here?"

J.W. said, "Yes."

"Okay."

She said the song was "Slow Dancing." If you lived in the seventies, you will know it. As they danced in a slow circle, others came and joined them.

She pulled away just so she could see his face. Then Miss Ginny kissed him.

As they kissed, he could smell her hair and the sweet scent of her skin, and he felt the way she felt in his arms for a moment or two. He forgot they were in a room full of people. The kiss ended as well as the dance. She gave him a look he hadn't seen from a woman in a long time.

J.W. asked if she would like another drink.

Miss Ginny said, "No, but I would like to see your place."

He replied, "It's nothing like yours."

Miss Ginny said, "I don't care. I want to see it."

"Okay. Where's your car?"

As they walked to the front, he saw the guys in suits were there again.

J. W. asked, "Do you ever go without these guys?"

Miss Ginny said, "Well, I kind of have to. I don't know the area, and they do, and they wouldn't let me."

Richard walked up and shook J.W.'s hand.

J.W. said, "Good to see you again. You must've felt a bit inconspicuous out here."

Richard smiled. "Just a bit."

"This is a rough bar." J.W. left a little. "It's my hangout. Nothing would happen to her here with me."

Richard replied, "That's the point, getting her with you."

J.W. realized this. "Oh, I see. Well, then, thank you for that."

Richard turned his attention to Miss Ginny. "Where do you want to go now?"

She looked over her shoulder at J.W. "I'm going with J.W. You all can go home."

J.W. said, "I'm not in my SSR."

Miss Ginny looked at him. "What are you driving?"

J.W. just pointed at the jeep. It looked like a beast in the parking lot.

J.W. said, "It has no top, and it's getting cool out here."

She turned back to Richard. "Bring me my coat, please. It's in the car."

"Yes, ma'am." He went to the car, got the coat, and came back.

Richard held it open for her to put it on. She said good night to Richard and then turned to J.W. "Okay, I'm ready." She was wearing a real fur coat from shoulder to ankles. "Okay, let's go."

They walked to the jeep. J.W. turned and swept her off her feet, put her in the jeep.

He thought, *I wish I had known she would wear that coat. I would've dusted off the seats, but too late now.*

J.W. said, "Okay, you have to hold on to the 'Jesus' bar, which is in front of you there. It is different from the 'Oh, sh———t' bar, which is above you, to the right."

He climbed in and started it up. One could feel the horsepower under the hood as they pulled out of the parking lot. He heard the tire holler. That's what big off-road tires do, car tires screech. And they were off to his house.

CHAPTER 6

Overnight Guest

Sunday night

As the tire hollered, she let out a great big laugh with one arm in the air and yelled, "Yeha, cowboy!"

She almost fell out of the jeep laughing. J.W. had to grab her to pull her back in. He was sure her security team cringed. He hit the on-ramp to I-44 west.

Ten minutes later, they were at J.W.'s house. He pulled up to the gate, pulled out the alarm remote to turn everything off, and opened the gate. He pulled in and up to the main door to the shop, opened it, and pulled in. He went around to help her out of the jeep. J.W. found her standing there with windblown hair and her shoes in her hand.

As she looked at J.W. with her hair dangling over one eye, she smiled like a teenage girl trying to get out of trouble with her boyfriend. It was cute and sexy. He guessed that was why it worked.

"Well, come on, you nut," J.W. said. "I will show you around. This is my shop."

She looked around. She saw the custom-built chopper with the skull headlight and matching air filter housing. She said, like a little girl, "I want to ride on that."

Then she saw the Harley Ultra Limited. "Oh, look, a bigger one."

"Okay, time to go inside." He closed and locked the shop, set its alarm, then turned to close the gate.

J.W. turned back. Rocky had her on the ground, licking her like crazy, and she was laughing, trying to hold him back.

J.W. yelled, "Rock, sit!"

Rocky did just as J.W. told him, and looked at him like "What?"

She finally sat up, still laughing.

J.W. asked, "Are you okay?"

She said, "I haven't had this much fun in years."

J.W. asked, "Are you drunk?"

She smiled. "Maybe. I don't know. I've never been!"

"Okay." J.W. walked over and scooped her and her things off the ground and took her inside. He called, "Come on, Rocky!" Rocky followed, tongue still out.

J.W. sat Miss Ginny in a chair as Rocky lay at her feet. J.W. gave her some water. He tried to straighten her up. She would wiggle her toes, and Rocky would lick them, and she would giggle.

J.W. was thinking, *I'm glad she doesn't have her little dog with her. Rocky might eat it.*

He went to get her a T-shirt of his. When he came back, she was on the couch with Rocky in her lap and was asleep.

J.W. said, "Okay, Rocky, get up." He didn't bring her home for Rocky.

The dog gave J.W. that look.

J.W. picked her up, took off her coat and then her jeans. He thought, *Cute undies.*

He left her shirt on but took off the bra. He put his oversized shirt on her and put her in the spare bedroom. Rocky joined her. J.W. looked at Rocky and said, "Traitor. Not that I blame you."

He walked down the hall. J.W. set the alarm and stripped down and got into bed. He lay there, thinking, *I bring a beautiful lady home, and the dog sleeps with her. I'm doing this wrong.*

He fell asleep.

He awoke to brutal sunlight.

J.W. got up to check on his guest. She was still out, with Rocky laying guard.

J.W. called softly, "Okay, boy, let's go outside."

The dog got up and ran outside. She didn't move. He walked over and checked her breathing.

Yep, still alive.

He went in to start breakfast: eggs and hash browns and a side of bacon with coffee. He was having a cup on the back porch when the dog came running out the back door, followed by Miss Ginny.

"Rocky, slow down before you kill yourself. Good morning. Would you like some coffee?"

She shook her head, then grabbed her head in pain.

"Just sit here." J.W. got a glass of water and two 800 mg ibuprofen. He handed her the pills and the water.

She took them and said, "How did I get this shirt on, and where are my bra and my pants?"

"They are all in the living room."

"Sorry about last night."

J.W. said, "You were having a ball."

She asked, "What's with this dog? He won't leave me alone."

J.W. replied, "Well, that's because he watched over you last night."

She asked, "And where were you?"

"I was in my bed."

She smiled.

He asked, "Can you eat?"

She replied, "I think so."

"Well, it's inside."

They sat at the table. Rocky lay at her feet. He dished up breakfast.

They ate. She would look like she wanted to say something, then didn't. She grabbed her milk and drank it all, then said, "This is hot!"

He said, "Oh, sorry about that. I forget sometimes about that. Eat the bacon and eggs."

She finished. He asked if she would like a shower.

She said, "Very much so."

J.W. took her down the hall, got her a fresh towel, and led her to the bathroom. He opened the door, let her in, and closed the door. About thirty minutes later, she came out with her hair in a towel.

J.W. asked, "Do you feel better?"

She said, "Much."

She was wearing his T-shirt and nothing more. J.W. was still in shorts and a tank top.

She reached out and grabbed his shirt and pulled him close to her. Down to her kiss. He could see her breasts weren't dry as they made the T-shirt see-through. As he kissed her, his hands went down to her ass.

He lifted her up and took her down the hall to his room. He walked into the room and shut the door on Rocky as he whined at the door. He pulled the shirt off her, and her body looked even better than he thought it would. As his arms wrapped around her, she loosened his shorts, and they hit the floor. All that could be heard was the thud of his gun.

She kissed down his chest. She lowered herself so she could take him in her mouth. He could feel the heat. She could also feel him getting harder and harder as it got to be too much.

He pulled her up and laid her on the bed so he could work his way up from her inner thigh. He kissed his way up to heaven. She began to moan, as her breathing became faster. He licked more and more. She began to move around the bed. He pulled her back to him. He felt her explode with feeling. He could feel her wetness again and again. He stood with her legs on his chest. He pulled her to the edge of the bed.

As he entered her, she gasped, and they began to move together— slow at first, then faster and faster. He erupted in her. They collapsed onto the bed, breathing heavily as sweat poured out of their bodies. She curled up to J. W. His arm went around her, and he pulled her closer. They drifted off to sleep.

The sound of the alarm woke them, still naked together in bed.

"It's 1 p.m.!" J.W. exclaimed.

He had to get ready for work, and she had to get ready to go home. He jumped into the shower and found she had joined him.

After the thirty-five-minute shower, he did feel cleaner but not much. He put on his work clothes. She got dressed.

J.W. got the SSR out of the shop and pulled it around front. He put the top down so they can enjoy the beautiful day. He drove her home.

Richard met them in the driveway. As he opened her door, J.W. told her he has to get to work, and can he see her again on Wednesday for dinner?

She smiled. "Call me. We will make plans."

He nodded and backed up. He hit the air horns and was down the hill.

*****

Richard asked, "Did you have a nice evening?"

She smiled that knowing smile. "I sure did, and the morning was even better."

She walked into the house like a dreaming schoolgirl.

Richard said, "That must've been some night."

*****

J.W. got to work just in time. He parked the SSR and got on the clock.

What a day.

CHAPTER 7

The Crash

Monday night

As J.W.'s shift came to an end, he walked out to the truck. It was a nice night: a few clouds and a soft breeze. He felt good.

J.W. heard a shot ring out. He automatically hit the dirt. He looked around. He saw the taillights of a Ferrari across the parking lot outside the fence across the postal parking lot.

It's that damn Ferrari again.

J.W. jumped up and ran to his truck. He hit the remote as he came around the back of the truck. He jumped in and fired that mother up. As he got to the end of the parking lot to the exit lane, the Ferrari passed at the other end about three hundred yards. He had to go through the gate and over a one-speed bump, then it was all pedal from there. At the end of the drive, he could see them turn left. J.W. had to slow down because that was the Oklahoma Highway Patrol office.

J.W. could gain some ground as he sped by the cops' shop; no one was there. He got to the far side of the on-ramp to I-44 west. The Ferrari had just gotten on as soon as J.W. got on the highway. It was a low-traffic night. He could see them about a half mile up.

J.W. hit the NOS and was moving. He was on the Ferrari in a second, and they knew it. They tried to lose J.W., but the SSR had more horsepower and J.W. had better driving skills. As J.W. was following him, he flashed a gun. J.W. pulled out his .45-70 handgun from its hiding place, just in case.

J.W. was still on the Ferrari's rear bumper. When they tried to take the I-44 to US-75 on ramp south at 103 mph, the Ferrari slid sideways, hit the curb, flipped three times, and landed on its roof. J.W. was able to stop on the on-ramp. He turned on his flashers to warn other drivers then walked up to the car slowly just in case.

J.W. could see a body. It was the tall thin man whom he had seen on the camera at his house. He was unconscious, with a deep gash to his forehead. J.W. put his gun away and pulled out the man from the wreck.

J.W. got the man to a safe distance. The police showed up as J. W. was checking the man's injuries.

The cop asked if he would be okay. J.W. told him to call an ambulance, and the cop did. J.W. told him to search the car for a gun. He did and found a chrome-plated .45.

The man came to, saw J.W., and started to struggle. J.W. pulled out his .45-70 and put it to the man's chest. The man stopped moving.

As the cop was coming back, he yelled at J.W., "Drop the weapon!"

J.W. told him, "Not till you have this man in custody."

The cop threw J.W. his cuffs, and J.W. put his gun down. Turned the man over and cuffed him. When the cop came closer, he looked at J.W.'s gun and said, "That's one big gun."

J.W. stood up, grabbed his new friend, and jerked him to his feet. The cop picked up his gun.

J.W. told him, "Thanks. I will get that from you later."

About that time, the car sparked and ignited the gasoline. The whole thing went up in a ball of fire. Luckily, they were just far enough away that it didn't get them.

As they put J.W.'s new friend in the back of the cruiser, the cop turned to J.W. and asked, "What the hell is going on here?"

The fire roared on. J.W. explained what happened tonight and how the bullet from that gun can be pulled from the wall at the postal service wall. The cop asked what J.W. was doing with a gun.

J.W. just looked at the cop and said, "This is Oklahoma."

J.W. handed him his concealed weapons license. The cop just groaned, scratched his head, and said, "Okay, this is my second question: why do you have such a big gun? A .45-70? That thing is a cannon."

J.W. just smiled. "I'm afraid of 1950 Buicks. They scare me."

The cop chuckled and handed J.W. back his .45-70. The cop, Officer Blunk, said he would be in touch with J.W., so J.W. gave him his card.

The cop asked, "So why did he shoot at you?"

J.W. had no idea. "Let's ask him."

The cop agreed. "Why not?"

He opened the door to the car and asked the man.

The man said, "Because he has been seeing my wife."

J.W. asked, "Who is your wife?"

He said, "Miss Ginny Nelson."

The cop asked, "And your name?"

"Scott Nelson."

The officer told him, "So you still can't shoot at people and race your car through Tulsa! Now you're going to jail, and if Mr. Santee presses charges, there will be more."

Scott just stared at J.W. Then he said, "I want to see my lawyer."

As J.W. closed the door, the cop said, "Well, you heard the man. So are you seeing his wife?"

J.W. replied, "If I am, I didn't know about it, but I will find out ASAP. Am I free to go?"

The cop said, "Yes. I have your info. Don't go far, but I do have one more question: how did you keep up with and, even better, catch that Ferrari?"

J.W. said, "That will have to stay a mystery for now."

J.W. jumped into his truck and cleared the NOS lines. He just smiled and waved. As J.W. fired up the truck, he thought the cop must be a car guy too because he perked up at the sound of the supercharger.

As J.W. pulled away, he called Miss Ginny.

She answered the phone.

"Hello, Miss Ginny, this is J.W. What is your last name?"

She said, "Brown. Why?"

"Some guy just tried to kill me in a black Ferrari named Scott Nelson. He claimed that you were married."

"Scott was my high school boyfriend, but we never married."

"Well, he seems to think so. He's on his way to jail. He took a shot at me as I was leaving work."

She asked, "Are you all right, J.W.?"

"I'm fine. He can't shoot worth a damn. As far as that goes, he can't drive very well either."

She said, "I haven't talked to him in twenty years."

J.W. said, "Well, he don't have the black Ferrari anymore. He killed it, and damn near himself. If I hadn't pulled him from the wreck, he might be dead now. I will call you tomorrow. I'm going home to sleep. Good night, Miss Ginny."

J.W. hung up the phone. The whole night's activities ran through his head. He finally said, "To hell with it." He put it all out of his head for a while.

J.W. got home, had a shot and a beer, and put two more in the ice bucket. He walked out to the hot tub.

He took the cover off it and took off his robe. He put his beer on the little table he kept out there and his gun with it. He didn't need any more surprises tonight. He lowered his body into the water. It felt good at 104 Fahrenheit. He was sitting there, drinking a beer, as Rocky wandered into the yard. J.W. was finally relaxing when the doorbell went off.

"Dammit," he said.

He got out, put his robe on, and, with gun in hand, answered the door. Yes! It was Miss Ginny in a long coat.

J.W. said, "Hello."

She let the coat open; there was very little on under that coat. He invited her to come in; she kissed him in the doorway. He put his arms around her. He lifted her up, and she wrapped her legs around him.

He carried her inside the house. When he put her down, she let the coat drop, but she forgot he doesn't live alone. Just about that time, Rocky cold-nosed her. She let out a yelp and jumped behind J. W. Rocky followed her, and they played "Chase around J.W."

He had to laugh.

She playfully said, "Are you going to help?"

"Why? This is his favorite game."

She giggled at Rocky. He licked the back of her leg, and she leaped into J.W.'s arms. Rocky tried to follow. J.W. turned, and Rocky bounded off J.W. He told him to sit, and he did. J.W. put Miss Ginny back down. Rocky didn't move. She just looked at Rocky and then at J.W.

"You have trained him well."

J.W. said, "Now go pet him. That's all he wants."

She walked over to him; he didn't move. She looked so cute in a red thong and matching push-up bra and red stilettos. She bent over to pet Rocky. Rocky gave J.W. a look.

J.W. thought, *How can I tell him no?*

Miss Ginny stood next to Rocky, rubbing his head. He leaned on her, then J.W. told him, "Okay."

He leaped forward and turned to look at her. She just stood there like a deer in headlights. Rocky waited for her to move and for J.W. to tell him okay. Rocky broke form and wiggled over to Miss Ginny all happy and wiggles, as she bent down to pet him. Rocky came up all tongue and licked the side of her face. She stood up with her hand on the side of her face that he licked and looked at J.W.

"Well, I think he likes you."

About that time, Rocky spun around, and his back hip hit her leg. She went down in a thud. J.W. rushed over to her. Rocky helped in his own way, licking her and having a ball.

"Okay, Rocky, that's enough," J.W. said.

J.W. lifted her to her feet. She was half-crying and half-laughing. She said, "This is not what I had planned."

She smiled, put her hand down to Rocky. He put his head there so she could scratch it. She hung on to J.W. and petted Rocky.

J.W. said, "Pretty outfit to play with the dog in."

She slapped his chest, then she put her head on his chest and squeezed him tight. Rocky was done and went and lay down.

J.W. said, "Well, my dog likes you, so I guess I will keep you, if that's all right with you."

She kissed J.W. He took that as a yes, and he carried her off to the bedroom. He laid her on the bed and said, "I will be right back."

About that time, Rocky came running into the room and jumped on the bed beside her. J.W. looked at him and said, "Not tonight, boy. Come on."

He walked into the living room with Rocky on his heels. He picked up her coat and draped it over a chair. He opened the back door to send Rocky out for a while. He grabbed the remote to his door to lock it. He walked back and set the alarm to the house, as Rocky looked at him through the glass with a look of "Damn, locked out again."

He walked back into the bedroom. She had two pillows propping her up, with one leg straight up with the stiletto half on. She got it loose, and J.W. took it off her foot. Her legs were soft and smooth. He rubbed them up and down.

As he went down the leg again, she pulled him down to her and kissed him. He remembered he was in the hot tub. So he pulled her up and took her bra off and then the thong. He turned, led her to the bedroom door. He got a second robe out and put it around her.

She smiled. "Kind of big."

"Well," J.W. said, "I'm not a little guy."

She found her hand in the sleeve. He took her hand and led her out to the alarm and disarmed it. They walked out the back door to the hot tub. He told Rocky, "No, go play." And Rocky did.

He held her robe as she slipped out of it and into the warm water He put their robes on the hook. He grabbed her a beer from the ice bucket, opened it, and handed it to her. He climbed in with her.

As she moved closer to him, she saw the gun with the laser.

He raised an eyebrow. "You just can't be too careful."

She turned and sat between his legs and leaned back against him. They saw Rocky chase the squirrels all around the yard as they sat and sipped their beers, enjoying the moment. She rubbed his thighs, as his hand lay across her breast on one then the other.

The night went by. After a while, she turned to kiss him. One thing led to another, and before they knew it, they had water splashing all over the place. They got out of the hot tub and went inside, her bare bottom in his left hand and the gun in the right. He turned off the lights and set the alarm again as they lay in each other's arms. They fell asleep.

Later, he was awoken in the best way by Miss Ginny as she continued to pleasure him like only a lady can. He reached down to finger her as she slowly moved up then down on him. He caressed her nipples then her bottom. After a while, he lifted her so he could pleasure her in the same way. He heard little moans from her and could feel her excitement grow.

They moved, and they changed positions from one to another as the night rolled on. The final position was her hanging on to the headboard on her knees as he was behind her, her hair in his hands. He pounded her again and again with his hips in until they collapsed on the bed in tangled sheets and sweet sweat pouring off them. She snuggled close as they spooned and drifted off to sleep again.

Later, he awoke to the smell of coffee and the sound of Rocky jumping on the bed to say good morning. Rocky hopped around the bed, stepping on J.W. and looking cute with his long ears flopping around. Then J.W. heard a sound in the kitchen and ran off to see what it was.

J.W. looked at his clock. It was almost noon. He's got to get up.

Miss Ginny came in with a cup of coffee for him. She handed him the cup and climbed in with J.W. She clicked on the TV.

There was a report on the crash he watched last night. As it went on, the reporter said, "A good Samaritan had pulled the man from the wreck…" and how the man was booked into jail and would be arraigned today.

She looked at J.W. with one eyebrow up. "Good Samaritan?"

He looked at her. "I don't know anything about it."

He walked into the bathroom to shower. He got out and shaved. She watched him as Rocky watched her.

J.W. asked, "Well, is your driver coming to get you, or am I taking you home?"

He got dressed.

She smiled. "Let's play hooky and stay here all day."

He smiled. "It's a nice thought, but I have a truck, bike, and dog depending on him. So which is it?"

She frowned. He would take her home.

He dropped her off. As he opened the door, she took his hand. She rose up, and she pulled him down to kiss her. What a kiss.

She walked to go inside. He couldn't keep his eyes off her sweet little backside all the way up the stairs and in the door. As she stepped through, she looked back at him and smiled.

About that time, Richard said, "It's hard to resist watching her, isn't it?"

J.W. jumped to the side. "Oh, hi, Richard. I didn't know you were there."

He smiled. "You were lost in her walk."

J.W. smiled as he put his hand out. "Well, I guess I was, or I know you have my back here on the property."

Richard said, "Oh, yeah. Oh, yeah, that's it." He shook J.W.'s hand.

J.W. said, "Well, I got to get to work. I will see you on Thursday at the gun range, okay?"

Richard replied, "You can count on it."

"I got to get to work." J.W. waved goodbye, got in his truck, and left.

CHAPTER 8

Stabbed in the Back

Tuesday morning

J.W. got to work on time. His boss, April, was glad to see he was okay after the police pulled the bullet out of the building and said it was aimed at J.W.

She started to worry about him; she's a good boss. It was another usual night.

J.W. awoke the next morning. He felt good as he sat on his back porch drinking coffee. He watched Rocky chase squirrels, run through the yard with him, hot on their trail. It was like a game they were playing.

J.W. looked at the gate. Something looked wrong.

There was a man with a gun. J.W. grabbed his Hi-Point 380 off the table and fired it. J.W. hit the gun, and it hit the man in the face.

J.W. got up to go after the man, but he was gone. He dropped the gun. J.W. walked in to call the police because he had fired his weapon inside the city limits.

The cop showed up to take the report two hours later; all the usual BS. Forty-five minutes later, J.W. was done. He was ready to go back to bed, but it was Monday. He had to go to work.

J.W. went in to do the 3S (sh——t, shower, and shave) so he can go to work.

J.W. got in his dually truck to go to work. Everything else was in the shop, locked up. With all the alarms armed, he drove to work.

He felt like he was being watched, so he took the clover-leaf all four turns twice. He found his follower in a black Chevy.

J.W. went on to work and parked way in the back, behind an RV. He thought, *Why drive an RV to work?*

He walked into the building and went to work. It was one of those nights: what could go wrong did go wrong.

Twelve hours later, J.W. was going home. As he got close to his truck, he saw the RV was rocking, and she was not being too quiet about what she was doing in there. J.W. got in his truck and fired it up. The RV stopped moving.

J.W. drove away. He had made sure to put his .45-70 in the truck, just in case.

He pulled out of the driveway at the P&DC and pulled out the .45-70 and laid it on his lap. At the end of the block, he saw the black Chevy. As he drove by, he saw the driver was sound asleep.

J.W. eased the truck up nose to nose with the car. He hit the high beams and the air horns, and scared the piss out of the occupant. He was trying to hit the brake and steer away, but nothing worked at this stage. It was the funniest thing J.W. ever saw. J.W. was laughing at the fool as he backed up the truck and drove to the Harvard sports bar to have a shot of Tarantula tequila and a George Killian's beer.

That should hit the spot.

As J.W. walked in, some of the regulars said hi.

Amber got his shot and beer as she put them down in front of him. She put her arms out for a hug. He hugged her. He could feel her back pop as she went limp for a moment.

She pulled away and smiled. "I've been waiting a week for you. Where have you been?"

J.W. said, "Just working a lot."

About that time, he felt someone behind him. J.W. stepped to the left. He could see a knife slide by where he was standing. With his right hand, he grabbed the wrist. J.W. turned the arm and twisted as the knife came out. He put his left hand down hard on the elbow, forcing the other man down.

J.W. grabbed the wrist and bent it in an angle it was not supposed to go. Now he was in an arm bar, and J.W. can control him.

He forced him down. J.W. put his foot on the man's neck while still holding the wrist high in the air.

About that time, the bouncer came over and was about to say something. J.W. gave him a look, and he shut up.

J.W. said, "Clear a path. I'm taking this outside."

The bouncer did what J.W. told him.

J.W. had the man by the wrist. He told the man to stand and walk.

"You move in any way J.W. doesn't like, I could break his wrist. Do you understand?"

The man nodded.

As they walked through the bar, no one said a word. He got outside.

J.W. threw the guy in a corner. "Why did you try to stab me?"

The bouncer watched from the doorway.

The guy said, "I ain't telling you sh——t."

J.W. hit him in the Adam's apple—not to crush it but to make him understand he was not playing with him. Once the man could breathe again, J.W. said, "Who sent you? Or do I need to impress upon you that I will hurt you really bad?"

The man's eyes started to bug out. "No! no! no! I will tell you. I don't know the guy, he just paid us to stab you, that's it."

"Who is *us*?"

"My cousin. When you grabbed me, he ran out."

J.W. asked, "What did the guy look like?"

The man said, "Blond dude in a black Chevy!"

J.W. said, "Okay, you can go."

The man cried out, "Just like that?"

"Yes, just like that. Wait, just one more question: what did his face look like?"

"He has a bruise on his face."

"It's okay," J.W. said. "Take off!"

J. W. turned to go back into the bar. The bouncer looked at him, started to say something, then stopped.

J.W. said, "Smart man."

He walked past him. J.W. sat at the bar thinking. He went over what he knew. *Some guy in a black Chevy that can't shoot or be stealthy is trying to kill me? Why?*

About that time, J.W.'s phone went off. It was Miss Ginny.

She asked if he was busy.

J.W. said, "Nope, just thinking as I drink a beer. What are you up to?"

She said, "I was thinking I'd like to go for another ride in your jeep. It was fun."

"I think that can be arranged. How about in the morning?"

"Sounds great."

"Okay, see you then."

She hung up.

J.W. thought, *Okay, now I'm getting up early. Time to go home.*

He turned around to the back of the bar, and he went out the back door.

He grabbed his gun out of its holster; he will not be an easy mark tonight. He walked back around the front of the bar, watching for anything unusual. He didn't see anyone, so he went home.

As he pulled up to his house, he watched the street. Then he went inside his house and back out the back door to unlock the gate mechanism, after pulling the dually inside the fence.

With the truck all put up, he went to bed.

CHAPTER 9

Off-Road Outdoors Recreation

At 7:00 a.m., J.W.'s alarm went off and scared Rocky, which meant Rocky jumped up and landed on J.W., and not in a good way.

J.W. thought, *This is not a good start for a Tuesday.*

He hit the shower while thinking he better take the .45-70, just in case. All showered and shaved, J.W. put on his black jeans and a sleeveless biker shirt, also black. He looked in the mirror, thinking he must be in a dark mood. He put his shoulder holster on and loaded the .45-70 in it, ten extra rounds in the counterweight. He was ready.

J.W. grabbed his jean jacket and went out back. Rocky damn near ran him over. He wanted to play.

"Not right now, boy, but why don't you ride along?"

As Rocky ran around the yard, J.W. opened the shop. When he fired up the jeep, Rocky ran over to the edge of the concrete drive and waited. J.W. pulled it out and stopped, and Rocky jumped in. J.W. went to lock everything up; when he came back out, J.W. had his harness in his hand. Rocky wiggled all over the back of the jeep; he knew he couldn't ride in the jeep without the harness. J.W. hooked him up and pulled out from the back yard. He locked the gate, and they were gone.

J.W. drove through town. Rocky had his face in the wind. J.W. would look back at him through the rearview mirror; his jowls were flapping in the wind. It made J.W. laugh.

They pulled into Miss Ginny's area and got some weird looks, but J.W. didn't give a damn.

As they pulled up, Richard was there to meet him. J.W. put out his hand. Rocky lunged at Richard, but the harness held him in place.

Richard looked a bit surprised. "I didn't see him in there."

Rocky liked to lie on the floor. J.W. turned to Rocky. "It's okay, boy."

Rocky looked at him. The hair on his back started to flatten as his tail started to wag a little bit.

J.W. told Richard, "It's okay. You can pet him now."

Richard was, like, "I don't think so." But he put his hand out, and Rocky licked it.

He was petting Rocky when Miss Ginny came out of the house in shorts and a T-shirt. As she got closer, Rocky saw her and went to that side of the jeep to see what she was doing. As he rubbed against her, she stood by the jeep. She rubbed Rocky's head, and J.W. helped her into the jeep.

She asked, "Where are we going?"

J.W. looked at her. "Wrong question. Where *aren't* we going is a smaller category."

She smiled. "Okay, let's go."

Rocky licked the side of her face, and she bursts into a giggle. J.W. jumped in the jeep, put it in gear, and away they went.

They went out about twenty miles to the keystone dam area just before J.W. pulled into the sand. He got out, locked in the hubs, and put it in four high. They were off.

They had fun bouncing all over the hillsides and trails. They no longer saw anyone else for a while. J.W. stopped and got the cooler from behind the back seat. He unhooked Rocky and let him run and play in the water and run in the sand. The spot he stopped in was surrounded by brush and tall grass.

J.W. handed Miss Ginny a cold beer. He walked over to pee.

She said, "That's not fair. Where am I supposed to pee?"

"Anywhere you want. There's no one around but us. If there was, Rocky would tell us."

He walked back to the jeep.

She said, "That's not the problem."

J.W. reached into the glove box and pulled out a roll of toilet paper. She gave him one of those looks a woman will when she wants one to think they were in trouble. Then she smiled at him, took the paper, and walked off. "No peeking."

J.W. sat on the tailgate of the jeep, drinking a beer from the cooler and watching Rocky run back and forth, having fun. He heard her trying to be quiet as she walked up alongside the jeep.

J.W. said, "Is there an elephant walking up beside the jeep?"

He turned to see her. Her mouth was wide open.

She said, "How in the hell did you hear me?"

J.W. said, "With all the other noise around here, that's easy. Rocky stopped and looked at you and then ran off, so it had to be you."

With a bewildered look on her face, she shook her head. "I give up."

She walked over to J.W. as he reached into the cooler to get a beer for her. She took it and held the end up. He twisted off the top.

She said, "You are a very talented man." She leaned in to kiss him.

He kissed her softly and lightly at first, and she moved closer into his arms. He can feel her hands on his jeans as she unzipped him and undid the button on his jeans He could smell her perfume and feel the taste of her kiss.

She kept pulling him closer to her, then she pulled away. He could feel her pull him out as her sweet lips first touched him all soft, and then he was in her mouth, hard and warm. She worked him up and down. He tried to pull her up to him, but she was not done. She kept going. He could feel the movement coming.

Just before he exploded in her sweet mouth, she stopped and stood up. He could see her shorts were no longer on as the sun glistened off her red hair and white skin. He raised her up and sat her on the tailgate. She raised her legs. He put his arms under her legs as she held on to his neck. He lifted her up off the jeep, as they stood as one. He lowered her on to him. He lifted and lowered; it went on and on. He lifted and pulled her down on to him hard. She moaned as her long red hair flew in the breeze.

He pulled her down one more time. He lowered her to the edge of the jeep and let her legs fall. He pulled her up and turned her around. Her red hair lay across her back. He pulled her to him as he kissed her neck. He entered her from the back. He could feel her starting to climax and pulled her to him. He entered her. He could feel her explode all over him. He could hear liquid hit the ground. He came too.

He let her go, and she fell to the edge of the jeep. He could see her knees shaking as he slowly pulled out of her. J.W. turned her to him. He kissed her turned-up face softly as he held her there. The wind wrapped around their bodies.

She held him close to her, and then she pushed him back and stood up. She reached for her shorts. She walked away as he pulled his pants back up and fixed his gig line. He sat down on the tailgate and drank what was left of his beer.

She finally came back. She looked surprised and bewildered at the same time. She came close to him; he sat her on his lap. He put his arms around her as they listened to the wind.

In a shaky voice, she said, "I've never met a man like you."

He could tell she had always been in control of any relationship except this one. She was in new territory and in way over her head. Her heart and body were telling her, but she was not ready yet.

He looked at his phone. He only had three more hours before he had to go to work.

He told her, "We only have an hour left till we have to go back."

She pulled from him and turned, then she hugged him—a full body squeeze.

She whispered in his ear, "I've never had anybody make my body do that before." Then she kissed him again.

He guessed she had found an answer in the wind, so he put her in the jeep and called Rocky. Rocky came from across the river.

"Just what I need, wet dog."

Rocky jumped into the jeep, and J.W. clipped on his harness. Miss Ginny was trying to keep the wet dog off her, but that wasn't working, so she just gave in. J.W. jumped in and fired up the jeep, and they bounced around the area for a while, then headed back.

They got to her house. Miss Ginny was a mess. Rocky had mudded her up good, and the jeep got her a few times too. J.W. helped her out; she was smiling again.

She said, "Look, J.W. I'm a mess and covered in mud. How can you look at me?"

He smiled. "Miss Ginny, you have never been more beautiful in my eyes."

As she looked at J.W., a wide smile slowly came to her face.

Her eyes shone, and she said, "You better get out of here and get ready for work."

J.W. just grinned. "Okay, off to work."

She was about to walk into the house when she ran over to J.W. and kissed him one more time. She ran into the house.

About that time, Richard walked up and said, "I don't think I have ever seen her so happy."

J.W. turned to look at him. "Really?"

"I have been around here a long time, and she has never acted like that. She walks around in a daze and as if she were walking on air."

"Thanks for the insight, but I got to wash a dog and get ready for work. I will catch you later."

Richard waved goodbye.

J.W. drove back to his place. He pulled up to the gate. Rocky started to growl, and the hair on his back was up. J.W. turned off the jeep and got out. He unlatched Rocky and let him go, as he pulled his .45-70 from its holster.

He looked around. He couldn't see anything wrong, so he left Rocky there and went into the house. The alarm was still set. He walked out the back door. He had seen something flash by the porch. He looked again.

It's the dog from next door.

There was a board down in the fence.

That's not by chance.

He unlocked the gate mechanism and let Rocky in. Rocky ran around the yard, but nothing. J.W. checked the shop alarms: they were still set. He unlocked the shop, pulled the jeep in and the

SSR out. He grabbed his portable drill and pulled out six three-inch screws to fix the fence.

That should hold them.

He put the tools away, pulled the truck out front, and locked everything up. "Come on, Rocky."

He got the two of them in the shower and all cleaned up. He dried Rocky off, and J.W. got dressed and went off to work.

Work was good, and the time went by quick. By the time he got home, he was done. He let Rocky out, and when he came in, he set the alarms. He called it a day.

CHAPTER 10

A Day at the Gun Range

Thursday

J.W. heard the alarm go off. It was 9:00 a.m., Rocky wanted to be let out as J.W. made coffee.

He thought, Ha, it's Thursday.

He jumped into the shower and got dressed. Then he called Richard. "Can you still go?"

Richard said, "I've been looking forward to this all week!"

"Okay. Do you want to meet me or have me pick you up?"

Richard said to pick him up at Miss Ginny's place.

J.W. went out to the shop and grabbed his cleaning box and six cans of ammo. He unlocked the gun safe and started to pull out pieces to shoot. J.W. took a long case down and opened it. He laid down the handguns in rows; he counted nine and two machine guns he was licensed for; an M11 and an Uzi machine gun.

That should do it.

He then pulled down a second case. He put a Henry .45-70 lever action rifle, a .50 cal sniper rifle, and a .308 heavy-barrel sniper rifle. J.W. locked the cases and put them in the dually. He came back for all the ammo, the handguns, as well as a box full of clips and put them in the truck. He then pulled out ammo for the rifles. He got a brick (a brick is a thousand rounds) for each.

That should do it.

He pulled the truck out front, set the alarm, and went to lock everything up. It was a nice day, so he left Rocky out in the backyard with food and water. J.W. planned to be back by 1:00 p.m., so Rocky should be okay.

As he got into the truck, J.W. put his .45-70 revolver in his lap. As he drove away, he didn't see the black Chevy anywhere on the way over.

J.W. pulled into the parking area. Richard came out with two cases, and one of his people had three ammo cans. J.W. got out.

Richard said, "Where do you want them, J.W.?"

"Put the cases in the back seat and the ammo in the bed."

As he opened the back door, he saw there were only two cases.

"I thought there would be more."

Richard loaded them. His man put the ammo in the back, called Richard over, and looked into the bed of the truck. They just whistled.

"Are we going to war?" Richard asked.

J.W. looked at him. "No, I thought you might want to shoot a few of mine."

Richard just looked at J.W. then back into the bed of the truck. J.W. realized Richard was not in a suit but in blue jeans and a jean shirt.

J.W. said, "I don't think I've ever seen you out of a suit."

Richard just smiled. "Just how many trucks do you have?"

"A few."

About that time, Miss Ginny came bouncing out and down the stairs. She smiled at J.W. "I didn't know we were doing anything today?"

J.W. smiled back at her. "We aren't. Richard and I are going out to the range to shoot."

She said, "That sounds like fun."

J.W. looked at Richard. He smiled back at J.W. and nodded.

J.W. said, "Okay, you can come, but under one condition: Richard is off duty today. He's here just to have fun with us. Agreed?"

She gave Richard a thank-you smile, took both their hands, and asked, "What do I need?"

They both looked at her and said at the same time, "Nothing."
They laughed.

"All right, everyone in the truck," J.W. said. "We are wasting daylight."

They waked over to the truck. They had to restack the cases so Richard could ride in the back passenger-side seat, behind Miss Ginny.

J.W. drove through town to the gun range. It is an outdoor range by the town of Wagner. It has a range of targets up to a thousand yards.

Richard laughed. "What are we shooting, howitzers?"

"Oh, you will see," J.W. said.

They did their paperwork and were given a number on the line. They had 13 (funny).

J.W. backed up to their tables. Each lane had three tables, one after the other: one for weapon inspection, one for weapon waiting, and the final table for loaded weapons and extra clips. There was a fourth table where one could shoot from. It was about six feet long and five feet wide, with three different shooting positions: the prone position (when lying on the ground), the sitting position, and the standing position.

They unloaded the ammo first.

J.W. had six ammo cans, three brick cans, and a box of clips. Richard had three ammo cans. They got the four gun cases, laid them on the first table, and opened them for inspection. The range safety man came over and inspected them for safety.

Once they were approved, just before J.W. opened his cases, he told Miss Ginny to watch Richard's face. J.W. could see in the cases. Richard looked like a kid at Christmas. Miss Ginny walked over and closed his mouth that was gaping open.

After they were approved, they could start to load clips and move weapons to table 2. J.W. closed the rifle case for now as they got to the line. They all had a weapon. Miss Ginny had a .357 mag that J.W. put thirty-eight rounds in for starters. Richard carried a .9 mm Beretta. J.W. had his .45-70 BFR revolver.

There were three lanes for shooters at this lane, so each had their own targets. They attached to a cable that ran on a motor, so they can run it out as far as they want to shoot, up to a thousand yards.

Miss Ginny was set at twenty-five meters, Richard set his at a hundred meters, and J.W. set his at three hundred meters. Richard and J.W. stood. Miss Ginny sat at the table. They gave her sandbags and a lesson in shooting. Miss Ginny had a fifty round box, Richard had ten clips, and J.W. had a box of twenty clips. Miss Ginny started shooting and hit some on the target. Most didn't, but she was having fun.

Richard was good. He was hitting most of what he aimed at. J.W. was doing okay, but he could only see the target, not the round holes.

When they were done shooting, they left all weapons on the bench till Richard inspected them to be empty. Then they pulled in the targets.

Miss Ginny's looked like Swiss cheese; the holes were all over the place. Richard's had steady, concentrated places, mostly on the head and chest. J.W.'s took longer to come in, being so far out. As the target got closer, Richard looked surprised to see the grouping in the head and heart; all were no bigger than a baseball. About that time, Richard asked if he could shoot the .45-70.

J.W. said, "Sure."

He loaded the old casings back in the box they came from and handed Richard a new box. Miss Ginny was putting up a new target, and J.W. got her another box of thirty-eight rounds. J.W. put the Beretta on the firing table. J.W. went back to his case, opened it, and took out a .41 mm Smith and Wesson. He walked back up.

Richard had hung J.W. a new target. J.W. loaded the revolver then he started shooting. Richard looked at J.W. after his first shot with the 45/70 revolver.

"Yep, he's in gun lust."

They kept shooting that morning until the group broke for lunch. As it turned out, Miss Ginny had a surprise for them. She had a caterer come out and set up lunch. They had set up in front of J.W.'s truck. They cleared off a table, and the three of them had a nice lunch.

Miss Ginny said, "They have beer if you want one."

They both said, "Guns and alcohol—bad mixture."

J.W. said, "Maybe when we are done."

About that time, Richard remembered the rifles. "We still have some rifles to shoot."

J.W. said, "Okay, but we put everything else away."

"Sounds good."

They put away all the handguns except the Uzi and the M11; they were for last. J.W. pulled the .45-70 lever action rifle out and gave it to Richard. The 308 he gave to Miss Ginny. He pulled up the foam separator and took out the .50 caliber sniper rifle.

Richard said, "I didn't see that!"

J.W. said, "Because you were not supposed to till now."

All three sat at the tables, set the sandbags, and sent out the targets. J.W. set Miss Ginny's and Richard's at five hundred meters, where their scopes started. J.W. set his at a thousand yards.

Richard said, "Good luck with that."

"We will see," J.W. said.

Both watched Miss Ginny hold the rifle tight to her shoulder. She pulled the trigger. The rifle bucked but not as bad as Richard thought it would. He levered in a round and fired. It kicked big time, and he felt it, but he fired again and again.

J.W. looked through the scope at the target. He lined up on the head, moved to the right a half inch on the target for the wind, and squeezed the trigger. As the round left the rifle, he could feel the recoil. The round hit home, dead center in the head. He put four more rounds down range. One could see the dust from the rounds fired on the hill behind the target.

When J.W. was done, he reeled the target back in. Miss Ginny had done well with the scope and the lessons. She got eight out of ten rounds in the chest area. Richard had a good shot grouping, but it was all in the head and chest.

They were talking, and J.W. was still reeling in his target. As it got close enough to see, Richard's mouth gaped open.

There on the head was a smiley face: two eyes, a nosehole, and a three-shot smile.

He looked at J.W. "Where did you learn to shoot like that?"

J.W. just smiled. "Military. You want a try?"

"Hell yeah!"

All shot another round, except Richard and J.W. traded weapons. J.W. loaded the .45-70. He put his target out to 750 meters, adjusted the scope, lined up, and fired all five rounds, one after the other in rapid fire. J.W. laid the rifle on the table and reeled in his target. When he could see it, he saw all five shots were in an area the size of a half dollar.

J.W. just looked at Richard. "I'm cheating. They're my rifles, and I grew up shooting this one. It's an old friend."

He wiped down the old Henry. He put it back in his case. He wiped down the .45-70 BFR revolver, reloaded it, and put it back in his shoulder holster. Miss Ginny and Richard put the caps on the scopes and wiped them down.

As they put everything away, Miss Ginny said, "Let's go, I will buy you two gentlemen a drink."

They looked at each other and then at her.

"We are not finished," J.W. said. "Far from it!"

She said, "Where? Not everything is loaded."

J.W. handed them net bags. "We have to pick up all the brass."

She looked at all the casings on the ground. "We will be here all night."

After about forty-five minutes, they had an ammo can and three net bags full.

J.W. said, "Okay, it's 1 p.m. I got time for a beer and to get you two back so I can get to work at three."

"Okay, let's go."

They drove through town, back to the Harvard sports bar. They walked in and got a table.

The waitress came over and then backed up. "Where have you three been? You smell."

"We have been shooting all day," J.W. said. "We need three shots of Tarantula tequila and three George Killian beers."

She said, "Okay. Do you want to sit outside?"

J.W. looked at her. "Sounds like a great idea."

They went outside and sat down, away from the others.

Miss Ginny said, "That was rude of her."

Richard said, "Well, she's right. We *do* smell of cordite."

She said, "What's cordite?"

J.W. said, "Gunpowder."

Miss Ginny said, "Oh, I see. We just don't notice."

As the shots and beers came, they toasted gunpowder's smell and drank their shots and beers.

J.W. said, "Well, not to seem rude, but I have to get ready for work and get you two home."

Richard answered, "It sounds like a good idea."

They looked at Miss Ginny, who was half-asleep in her chair. J.W. paid the tab and picked up Miss Ginny. He carried her to the truck. She was worn out.

As he took them back, two of Richard's men met them at the truck. Richard pointed out his cases and gear as they unloaded. He came and got Miss Ginny.

J.W. said, "I can take her up."

Richard said, "You got to get to work. We will have to go again."

"Sounds good," said J.W.

Richard closed the doors, and J.W. drove off, back to his house. He got there and unlocked the gate mechanism and drove in. He opened the shop, put all the ammunition and cases upstairs in the office, and locked it, setting the alarms. J.W. pulled the SSR out front and locked the gates.

Rocky was so happy, he just kept bounding around the house. J.W. got in the shower and then got dressed. He set the alarms and left for work. He got there just in time.

All the guys kept saying, "Out shooting today?"

The women were talking about that strange smell.

J.W. said, "Guess it don't wash off that easy."

After work, he stopped by the Harvard and had a shot and a beer.

Amber said, "I hear you smelled to high heaven today."

J.W. said, "Well, that happens when you go shooting."

"Where's my hug?"

"Are you sure you want one?"

She hugged J.W. "You do still smell a little."

J.W. said, "I'm fixing to take care of that. Sorry, I got to go."

He got home, let Rocky out, got undressed, and climbed into the hot tub to just soak for a while. After about an hour, he dried off and went to bed.

The next morning, J.W. awoke fresh and felt pretty good, so he got something to eat and started setting up to clean his guns. He set up three fold-up tables with brown cloth towels and a hot-water metal trash can. After being all set up, there was a knock at the door. J.W. opened it. It was Richard.

Richard said, "Hi. I came by to help clean all the weapons."

"You're just in time." J.W. locked the front door.

Rocky came in the back.

"It's okay," J.W. said, as Rocky burst into wiggles. They walked out back.

Richard said, "You weren't kidding."

They got the two cases out and put them on table 1.

J.W. said, "We take off all grips and guards, then put them on table 2, where we dip them in the hot water to clean away the carbon. Then table 3, blow them dry, and leave them on table 3."

In about thirty minutes, they were done.

"Now they go from table 3 to 1," J.W. said. "On 3, we blow them off again and move to table 2. There we oil them with brake-free, then towel-wipe them down and move to table 1 to reassemble. We then put them in the safe."

The whole thing took an hour and twenty minutes, including taking care of tables and cans.

They sat on the back porch drinking a beer.

Richard said, "I thought that would take all day."

J.W. said, "I will run a rod down them tomorrow just to lube the barrels."

Richard smiled. "You're a very efficient man."

J.W. said, "Why do it the hard way?"

CHAPTER 11

Sweet Kiss at the Bar

Friday afternoon

They talked the rest of the morning about trucks and firearms, then J.W. walked Richard out to the shop.

"Now you have seen my shop."

Richard said, "Yes, it's very nice."

J.W. said, "Well, thank you. Come in the back room."

J.W. walked to the doorway, opened the door, and flipped on the lights. Richard's eyes got big and bright as he looked at J.W.'s motorcycle collection. There was everything, from an ATC 90 to a 45 Indian and a lot in between. There was a 1999 drifter, a 1980 XT500, a 2012 Ultra classic limited. Bob, his chopper, as well as a Bultaco dirt bike. Ossa trials bike and others in restoration.

Richard just stared at all of them, then he turned to J.W. "Do you ride them?"

J.W. said, "I drive or ride every vehicle on the property. Restoring and building bikes and trucks are hobbies."

"How long have you been doing this?"

"Well, I had that three-wheeler in high school and the XT500. I've kept everything I have ever purchased, and after a while, I restore them."

Richard said, "But they all look new."

J.W. said, "Isn't that the point of restoring?"

"Well, I guess."

"But it's still a little cool to ride just yet, but soon! What, do you think I don't have a truck?"

They both laughed. J.W. locked up the shop and set the alarms. They walked back to the porch and had one more beer and talked bikes.

Richard knew quite a lot about bikes; his dad was a flat tracker, so he grew up around bikes.

After a while, J.W. asked him if he had one.

Richard said, "I do, in Texas. I just haven't had enough time to go get it, but I got some time coming."

"What is it?"

"It's a Hayabusa."

J.W. said, "You can kill yourself on one of those. That's like strapping yourself to a bullet! Too fast for my old body. I'd like to live longer."

Richard said, "Yeah, they're fast, but they handle nice."

"Okay, I will take your word for it. Not to be rude, but I have to get ready for work. Thanks for the help cleaning. You helping made it a lot faster."

"After all, I shot yours more than mine."

They shook hands. Richard walked to his car. J.W. locked the front door and called Rocky in. J.W. locked the back door and set the alarm for the doors and windows, but not the motion sensors. He walked into the bedroom, Rocky lying across the bed.

J.W. said, "And what are you doing?"

Rocky looked at him, his nub of a tail wagging as fast as it can, then he just flopped back down. Patiently chasing squirrels all morning was tiring. In minutes, he was snoring.

J. W. jumped into the shower and shaved. As he was getting dressed, his phone rang. It was Miss Ginny, wanting to know what he was doing on a Friday night.

J.W. said, "I'm only doing one thing."

"Oh, what would that be?" she said, all sexy-like.

He let her have it.

J.W. said, "I'm going to work."

There was silence, then pure joyful laughter.

When she was done, she said, "I had all kinds of things turning through my brain, going to work never crossed my mind." She giggled again.

Okay, after work, he would probably stop at the Harvard sports bar and have a few.

She asked, "About what time?"

"Oh, about 11:30."

Can she come see him? He would love it.

He hung up the phone and set the alarm and left Rocky having puppy dreams as he was running in his sleep. J.W. was off to work. The wind was kicking up again. But then again, this was Oklahoma. Hell, the wind was even in the song "Oklahoma." So it had been around for a while.

As he got to work, he was glad he took the dually. Between trash can lids and everything else the wind threw around had half-hit the truck.

He was here now. As he walked in, his boss, April, was standing just inside the door.

J.W. asked, "Are you waiting for me?"

She gave him a look of "What J.W. said didn't register."

Then he guessed it. It clicked. "Oooh, no, not you."

J.W. thought she worked too hard, but she's the best boss he'd ever had. Always up on things and sharp as a tack, but mostly, she treated people with respect, and he liked that.

J.W. walked to where he clocks in and did so; got his duty assignment. He was in the DBCS again. He didn't mind. They were fun to work on.

About 7:00 p.m., he had some lunch. He drove to Subway for a pizza; they were pretty good, with plenty of jalapenos. After a good lunch, back to the DBC machines and TMS towers for him. Only four hours to go, then beer 30.

They went by fast, and he clocked out. Off to the bar.

As he pulled up, he saw the lot was full. He parked way out in the back and walked in.

The bouncer shook his hand and said, "Have fun, it's a nice crowd."

As J.W. got to the end of the bar, he saw a man and woman were leaving. He thought, *Good timing.*

As he sat down, a pair of lips kissed the side of his neck.

He looked, but all he saw was some guy who had his back to him.

What the hell?

As he looked at Amber, she smiled and looked past him. J.W. turned to see Miss Ginny playing with him.

"Okay, girl."

About that time, the guy next to him turned around. It was Richard.

J.W. looked at him. "Aw, dude, I damn near hit you."

He laughed at J.W. He saw what she had been doing, so Richard turned on purpose. He figured it was the safest move. Well, it worked.

Amber walked up.

J.W. said, "A round for all three."

She pulled out three shot glasses and the Tarantula tequila and three Killian's beers. They toasted to the military.

"May they all come home safe."

They downed the shots. Friends would come by and say hi.

As a band J.W. liked started to play again, he told his friends, "This is Under the Gun. They play great country and classic rock. They are my favorite band in town."

They listened to the band and drank their beers. After about four or five rounds later, the band was done for the night and came over to say hi. J.W. got them a round, and Peewee tried his best to flirt with Miss Ginny. After a few minutes, she just put her arms around J.W., and he got the idea. Peewee was not worried; he had a whole fan club hanging around.

After a while, it was time to go, but J.W. was in no condition to drive.

Miss Ginny said, "Come to my house. Leave your truck here."

He couldn't. He has a dog counting on him.

Miss Ginny said, "Well, we will pick him up. Okay, who's driving?"

Richard looked at J.W. and said with a humorous smile, "The driver."

About that time, a long limo pulled up, and two men got out.

J.W. told Richard he couldn't leave the truck. It had guns in it.

Richard said, "Okay, give me the keys."

J.W. did. He pointed it out, and Richard walked over to one of his men and pointed out the truck. The man walked over to it, unlocked the truck, and climbed in. He pulled in behind the limo.

They pulled out. They were on the way to J.W.'s house. Miss Ginny reached into a drawer and pulled out three beers.

J.W. looked at her. "That's a cool trick."

Richard laughed. "It's a mini fridge for beer or wine."

He pushed a button. A panel opened, and a whole bar came out, with glasses on the other side and ice.

Richard just smiled. As they got to J.W.'s house, they saw the black Chevy was at the end of the street.

There was that damn Chevy again. J.W. didn't know what that guy's problem was, but he was going to get him.

Richard locked the doors and told his men, "Go check that truck out." He then looked at J.W. They had been drinking. "No chasing bad guys for us."

J.W. knew Richard was right. About that time, the Chevy did a rear slide and took off down the back street. The men came back, checked out the house. All clear. They got out, and J.W. went to get Rocky, who was not happy with all these strange men everywhere.

J.W. looked around. Everything was good, so J.W. let Rocky out front, set the alarm, and walked out. Rocky saw Miss Ginny and was all over her.

J.W. said, "I think he just might like you."

She climbed back in the limo. Rocky looked at J.W., waiting for permission to follow her.

"Okay, boy, get in."

Richard, with the door. "After you. I'm taking no chances with him."

J.W. said, "Okay, I will get in first."

As he got in, there was Miss Ginny with a lap full of boxer. She was just lovin' on him, and Rocky was in hog heaven.

Richard looked at J.W. "Think you lost your girl."

J.W. replied, "It wouldn't be the first time too."

They were off to Miss Ginny's place. As they pulled up, J.W. saw his truck had made it and the keys were in the house. They stopped, and Rocky woke up. As Richard and J.W. got out, Rocky damn near ran them over to get outside. J.W. stood up and turned to help Miss Ginny out. He was sobering up a little.

They turned to see where Rocky had gone. He was running around the whole yard, which was very large. After a while, he came back and peed on the grass.

Thanks, Rocky.

They walked to the house. Richard went to his room, and Rocky fell in-step with them. The front door opened, and Michelle was standing with two cold beers.

About that time, Rocky walked up to her. She didn't know what to do. J.W. called him back to him ("With me"). He looked up and walked with J.W. As they came through the door, J.W. introduced Michelle to Rocky in a very polite manner.

She said, "Hello, Rocky. Welcome."

She handed them a beer. It was really cold. J.W. opened his and handed it to Miss Ginny. He took hers and opened it, then J.W. asked her, "Okay, now that you got me here on your home turf, what shall we do now?"

She gave him a sly smile. "Guess you will have to follow me."

She walked across the huge room. They followed her. Rocky walked with J.W.

They walked down a long hall. She stopped and opened a door. He walked in; it was a game room.

She smiled. "Do you play pool?"

He replied, "Have been known to play."

She racked the balls. He told Rocky to lie down and be good. He sniffed around a bit and laid down by the door.

As they were playing the second game, someone came down the hall. Rocky was on his feet, growling. J.W. called Rocky over to him.

Moments later, a knock at the door, light and gentle.

Miss Ginny said, "Come in."

It was Michelle.

J.W. told Rocky, "It's okay."

He was all wiggles.

Michelle asked, "Will there be anything else?" She looked at J.W. "Another beer?"

"No, thank you. This is the most I've drunk in a long time."

Michelle turned to leave, but Rocky was blocking her path.

"He just wants you to pet him," J.W. said.

She said, "Yes, sir."

"You don't have to. It's just the way he senses if you're good or evil."

She looked at J.W. with indignation. "Sir, I am not evil. I know you. You just raised your voice to me, and you're still standing."

With a confused look on his face, J.W. said, "He's trained as a bodyguard for me. See, he is still wagging his tail. He thinks you are okay, and that's good enough for me. You may call me J.W. And I don't want to hear *sir* anymore, Miss Michelle. We are friends now."

Miss Ginny smiled. "Would you care to join us in a game of pool?"

Now she looked confused. "Ma'am?"

"You have been with me so long I think of you that way, and have for a while. Will you please stay for a game or two?"

"Certainly, Miss Ginny."

"It's Miss Ginny when no one else is around."

"Thank you, Miss Ginny. I would love to play with both of you."

They played pool for an hour or two.

Michelle said, "I have to go. Have to be up early in the morning."

"But it's your day off."

"Yes, I have a hair appointment at nine."

"Good night, Miss Michelle. Sleep well. Speaking of sleep, I'm ready to get some myself."

Miss Ginny took J.W. by the hand. With Rocky following, they went off to her room. Rocky came in. J.W. looked around. The bedroom was as big as his shop. He could get seven cars in there and walk around them. She sure liked open rooms. There was a fireplace and a balcony outside the door.

J.W. asked, "Can I use the restroom?"

"It's in there."

He walked in; it was half the size of the bedroom! Well, he did his business and washed his hands.

As J.W. walked back in, Rocky was asleep on a plush rug, and Miss Ginny was in bed, sound asleep. As he climbed in, she snuggled close and pulled his arm around her, and they both fell asleep, spooning.

CHAPTER 12

Riding Horses

Saturday morning

As J.W. awoke, he heard a little dog barking. When he opened his eyes, J.W. remembered where he was.

Miss Ginny was not there, but her place in the bed was still warm.

Where is that barking coming from?

J.W. got out of bed. He could see Rocky was lying flat on the floor so he could play with her little Taco Bell dog. It was funny to watch, but he had to go.

J.W. walked to the bathroom and did what he needed to. When he came out, all his clothes were gone and his things were on a small table, including his gun and holster. He bet she had fun playing with that. Well, everything was here. Okay, he was standing in her bedroom with no clothing.

Great, now what?

He stood there thinking. Rocky came over to J. W. He wanted to be outside. J.W. looked around the room; he found a white terry cloth robe, and put it on and his boots.

As he was about to walk out, Miss Ginny walked in with a tray of food. She looked at him and started giggling. The robe barely fit. Here he was, cowboy boots, white robe, and cowboy hat. She was giggling at him, and the dog had to pee. His day was not starting well.

She stopped giggling. "Where are you going in that outfit?"

"Where are my clothes?"

She just smiled, and the room got brighter. "They are being washed. They smell like smoke."

"Well, Rocky has to go out."

"We will take him together."

They stepped into the hall with both dogs, and J.W. found an outfit. They were off to go outside. As they stood on the back deck, the dogs went out in the grass. After they were done, Rocky just ran around as her little dog tried to keep up with him.

With Miss Ginny on his arm and the dogs running, J.W. could smell the start of spring. Soon, it will be bike season. Soon, it will be loud pipes and rally time. J.W. did love spring.

They were watching the dogs play. Michelle brought out some coffee. It smelled good, but it was in small cups.

Michelle asked, "Is everything all right?"

"I thought you had a hair appointment," said J.W.

Michelle said, "I was just heading out, thought you would like coffee, J.W."

"Thank you."

She had seen J.W. palm the cup.

She could see he was having trouble with the cup. She then pulled a white napkin off a coffee mug, and she smiled.

Michelle said, "I had a feeling."

J.W. said, "Thank you, Michelle. That's more like it."

She handed J.W. the mug and took the little china cup. She stepped back. She looked at what J.W. was wearing. "I need to get you a bigger robe, but you pull off that outfit." She smiled.

He knew she was kidding him.

She walked inside. Miss Ginny agreed with Michelle.

J.W. stood there in the spring breeze, drinking his coffee. She started giggling again. J.W. didn't look at her; like he didn't know she was there. Then she started laughing wholeheartedly, and then he could see why. Her little dog was sitting next to him like it was on guard duty, and Rocky was on the other side doing the same. The three of them just stood there looking out over the land.

Miss Ginny lost it. She was laughing so hard she had to sit down. There were tears running down her face. None of them moved. J.W. drank his coffee in his fluffy white terry cloth robe, cowboy hat, and boots.

She called her little dog, but it didn't move until J.W. was done with his coffee.

J.W. said, "Okay, let's go inside."

Both dogs broke and ran for the door.

Miss Ginny, still giggling, said, "If I only had a camera. That was too funny. You looked like you were born here with all your dignity. You are quite a man, J.W."

A few of the maids stepped out of rooms and waited for them to pass. J.W. was sure they were thinking, *Who is this guy?*

As they got back to her room, they saw J.W.'s clothes were back. They lay on the bed eating the food she had brought earlier.

After a while, J.W. said, "Let's do something."

Miss Ginny said, "Okay, what?"

"Do you have any horses?"

"Yes, we do."

"Great! We can go riding before we go out tonight."

"Sounds good to me."

"Okay," J.W. said. "I'm in the shower."

"Or we can take a bath together."

"Even better."

As she went in to start a bath, J.W. checked his phone. No alarms or messages.

He heard her call, "It's ready."

J.W. walked in to find her in the tub up to her ears in bubbles. He thought, *Ha, bubbles. More girly stuff.*

He climbed in; it was warm and soapy. J.W. sat down, and she started washing him. J.W. had never had this done before, and it felt good.

After about thirty minutes, they got out. Every place on both their bodies was clean now. They got dressed to go riding.

J.W. walked out to his truck and got his riding boots with WWI military brass spurs. Miss Ginny came out in preppy-style riding gear with a helmet. J.W. pulled the seat forward so he could get his chaps. He buckled them on. "Now I'm ready to ride."

J.W. came around the side of the truck.

She stopped and stared at him. "Where did you get them boots and chaps from?"

J.W. said, "My truck. I keep them in there."

"You look like you stepped out of a movie."

About that time, a man showed in a golf cart built for eight people.

She said, "Climb in."

Miss Ginny and J.W. got in behind the driver. Rocky wasn't sure about the golf cart, but he lay on the floor behind them. The driver took them to the stables. As they got there, two horses were saddled and ready, but they were English saddles.

J.W. looked at the man who brought them out. "Do you have a Western saddle?"

He said, "Yes, but it's a 16."

"Perfect, that's my size." As he got it, J.W. took off the other saddle, placed it in the saddle tree, and grabbed a saddle blanket.

Rocky tried to smell the horses and got snorted at. So he went over and laid in the grass. As the man came out, he put it on the horse.

He stepped back, and J.W. adjusted the saddle to where it should be. The man handed J.W. the girth strap. He looped the leather strap through, pulled and looped it again, pulled and looped one last time. The horse tried to hold its breath so it won't be tight enough. J.W. waited for him to breathe again and pulled it tight. He got all the slack out and pulled it through the buckle. When adjusted, the stirrups strap. They were close to where he needed them, and he climbed on.

The man—Chett was his name—helped with final adjustments.

"Okay, Chett, what's the book on him?" J.W. asked.

Chett look surprised. "'The book' is a rodeo term most people out of the circuit would not know." He looked at J.W. "You ride?"

J.W. had ridden the circuit a few years back when he was young, and then he told him "the book." "If you ease him out, he does fine, and he spooks at plastic bags."

"Most horses do."

"Okay."

Miss Ginny was mounted, and J.W. called Rocky.

They were off to see the hills of Barry. They rode for about an hour. The horse was not too crazy about Rocky at first but got used to him. They pulled up at a pond, where Rocky jumped right in and swam around for a while as the horse drank. They talked about where she grew up and her mom. J.W. told her about the ranch back home in California, outside San Diego.

She asked why he was in Oklahoma. Last duty station was Fort Sill. Then got work up here.

They walked along the pond.

An old man walked up. "Y'all know this is private property."

Miss Ginny popped out from behind her horse. "Why, yes, I do."

"Oh, ma'am, I didn't see you." His name was Davey, and he took care of this side of the property.

"How far does it go?"

"It's actually many properties divided by public land. We get people here without permission once in a while. It drives him crazy."

"It sure does."

"Well, are you ready to ride back?"

They took a shortcut, and in twenty minutes, they were back.

Chett took the horse. "I looked you up, Mr. Santee. You made the IFR two times."

J.W. said, "That was a long time ago."

He replied, "Well, I never made it that far."

J.W. said, "You know, it's all in the luck of the draw."

The old man said, "Ain't that the truth."

"Besides, it looks like you did all right: nice stables, lucked into this job. Bet the pay is good and the room is nice. No one can ask for more than that."

"Ain't that the truth. It was nice meeting you."

"Next time," J.W. said. "I will bring my saddle, and all three of us will ride."

"Sounds good. Bye."

J.W. looked for Rocky. Rocky was rolling on the grass, and the sprinklers were on. They got back on the cart, wet dog and all.

Back at the truck, J.W. put Rocky in the back seat after he put things away. He kissed Miss Ginny and got into his truck.

J.W. said, "I will be back at nine."

She said, "Why don't we take the limo tonight so we can have fun like last night?"

"Okay. About nine?"

"Sure. See you then."

He drove home. All he could smell was lake-water dog mixed with wet dog all the way home. He pulled up into the driveway and parked and left the windows down so the smell could get out. J.W. took Rocky into the house and checked everything. All secure.

He got Rocky and himself in the shower and all cleaned up. He shaved, put some Stetson cologne on, walked into the bedroom, and pulled out black Wranglers and a white brushpopper shirt and belt. He pulled out a box from under the bed; inside was a pair of well-made black boots with silver tips.

After J.W. got dressed, he took a box down off the shelf in the closet and opened it. Inside the plastic bag was a one-trick black hat with a silver band. He reached into the closet and pulled out a suit bag. Inside was his long frock black coat. He hung that on the door. On the top dresser drawer in a box was an Indian dance bolo in turquoise jet coral. His father made it years ago. It was one of the favorite things his dad gave him. Forty years later, the bolo still looked great.

He put it on. J.W. heard Rocky barking to let him know someone was outside. J.W. slipped on the jacket, checking the mirror.

Well, this is the best you can do? Hope she likes it.

There was a knock at the front door. He answered it.

Richard was there. "We are here."

J.W. said, "Okay. Let Rocky out, and I will be right there."

J.W. got his wallet and keys. Rocky came into the house. J.W. set the alarm, opened the door, and left. He got to the car. She was wearing a white dress with sparkly stuff everywhere. Her hair was down in long waves of red; she was flat-out gorgeous. J.W. figured he better dress up a bit. "Where do you want to go?"

"Anywhere you want. Do you have a membership to the club in the B of A building downtown?"

"Why, yes, and some of my friends are there tonight," J.W. said. "I've always wanted to go there. I've heard the view is beautiful at night."

Miss Ginny said, "You want to go to see the view?"

"Yes, why else go?"

"Okay, let's go."

The driver drove them downtown to the Bank of America building. There were four doormen in blue jackets and tan khakis. She signed them in, and they entered the elevator. It took them to the top floor, seventy stories up. They stepped out of the elevator. A man directed them to the coat check. She checked her coat, and they walked in. She took J.W.'s arm. He could hear the talk increase.

They made their way to the bar. J.W. knew they would not have George Killian beer or Tarantula tequila, so he ordered a bourbon and Dr. Pepper. She had wine.

As they turned around, three women walked up to Miss Ginny.

"How have you been? We haven't seen you in ages."

J.W. excused himself so the ladies could talk. He walked over to the windows. *You can see the whole city from up here.*

He looked at the lights and drank his drink.

Miss Ginny joined him. "You weren't kidding about the view, were you?"

J.W. was looking to the west. She took his hand and said, "Let's dance."

A small three-piece band was in the corner playing something slow, like in the forties.

They had a good sound. As they danced, the lights would hit the dress she was wearing, and little light would be all around them.

As she melted into his chest, they danced in small circles till the song was over.

A tall woman came to the microphone to sing; she had a soft, smoky voice. J.W. held his hand out. Miss Ginny took it and moved into his arms as the woman sang. The room seemed to disappear. It was just her and him on the dance floor.

At the end of the song, J.W. excused himself and walked over to the woman singer. He told her she had a voice as smooth as silk and he enjoyed it very much. "Thank you for singing."

He turned to walk back to Miss Ginny. She was talking to a tall man, about six feet or six feet one. As he got closer, she cried, "You're hurting my arm."

J.W. then moved in fast and caught him by surprise. He took his hand off Miss Ginny's arm, bent his wrist in, and pulled him in close. With his elbow on the inside of J.W.'s arm, he had his wrist and thumb bent to his advantage. The guy was in pain.

J.W. whispered in his ear, "The lady is with me. You touch her again, I will break every bone in your body. Now tell the two dime-store goons coming this way that you're okay, or I will break your wrist and your face before I kill both of them."

About that time, Richard stepped out of the shadows in front of the two men and held his hand up. They stopped, and he turned around and watched J.W. The two men looked confused but didn't move. J.W. looked back at Miss Ginny, who was rubbing her arm.

J.W. said in a low voice, "If she bruises, I will put the same on you. Do I make myself clear?"

The man nodded his head up and down. About that time, Miss Ginny looked up and saw the situation. She gave a sly smile. "J.W., please don't hurt him. He's my brother."

J.W. looked at him and said, "Apologize."

He looked at J.W. with an indictment. "I will not."

The next thing, he was up on his tiptoes with tears in his eyes. "Are you ready now?"

He cried out, "I'm sorry."

J.W. let some pressure off his wrist. Her brother was mad, and there was nothing he could do about it.

Miss Ginny said, "Mark, I would listen to J.W."

She looked around the room. No one had noticed the altercation. She looked back at him. "You see, no one is watching yet. If you don't give me a real apology, I will let him beat the crap out of you in front of all your friends. Is that clear?"

J.W. loosened up on Mark so Mark wasn't on his toes anymore. Mark then gave a sincere apology.

"J.W., you can let him go."

He did. Mark was really pissed off now. Just before J.W. walked away, he looked at her arm. It was starting to bruise. Five dark fingers.

Miss Ginny went to take J.W.'s arm, but he moved just out of her range. As Mark turned to say something to Miss Ginny, J.W. hit him with a solid left. His head popped to the left and spun around. As he lined up, J.W. hit him square in his right shoulder, sending him flying across the room.

As he hit the floor, he slid up to the singer's feet. The singer looked at J.W., nodded, and started another song. As he turned back to Miss Ginny, she smiled at him.

J.W. said, "I told him if you bruised I would do the same to him and your bruising. I didn't want him to think I was a liar."

She giggled and took his arm. As they walked to the bar, Miss Ginny said, "Bill me."

The man said, "Yes, ma'am."

They walked to the coat check.

Richard stood there, just smiling. Then he told the two men to go get their boss and not to worry, he had them covered.

As they stepped in to the elevator, the chatter started again. Richard stepped in too.

"Okay, what's with the sh——t-eating grin?" J.W. asked.

Richard kept smiling. "May I, Miss Ginny?"

She said, "Please do. I have waited years to see that."

J.W. said, "Seen you stop the goons."

"That was for their safety, not yours."

"Well, they won't get into trouble, they work for me," Richard said. "He was out cold, and you're faster than you look."

Miss Ginny squeezed J.W.'s arm.

Richard said, "I knew if he was there he would try to bully you, so I had to watch. So where to now? The Harvard?"

"Yes, sir."

As they got to the limo, an ambulance was pulling up.

"Well, he has medical attention now. I don't think they can fix his pride."

They all started laughing.

They got to the Harvard, and the place was buzzing! They walked in, and the bouncer looked at them. "Are you sure you want to wear clothes like that in here?"

J.W. just smiled. "Hell yes."

They walked through the crowd to the corner. He liked the way people moved over and let them have a seat.

Ashley, J.W.'s favorite waitress, came over. "Whoa, don't you too look sharp?" She hugged J.W. and Miss Ginny. "Beer and a shot?"

Miss Ginny said, "Make it two."

Ashley had words tattooed all over her shoulders. They looked nice, and she had a smile that can light up a room. She used it to get good tips. Her counterpart was Alyssa, the bartender. Together, they were a lot of fun, and they kept the party jumping.

Alyssa put the drinks on the bar. "Hi, J.W. Welcome back in." She was off to serve someone else.

The band was okay. When they took a break, J.W. put a few bucks in the jukebox, and he took Miss Ginny out on the small dance floor. They danced a one-step, and he dipped her. She almost came out of the top of her dress. He turned her away from the crowd.

Using J.W. as a blocker, she straightened things out.

"Sorry about that," J.W. said.

She giggled. "I don't think this dress was made to do that."

They turned back around.

J. W. said, "I don't think that guy in the front chair will ever be the same."

She slapped his chest. "Stop it!"

They danced three more songs, and the band was about to start again. They went back to their drinks.

Ashley said, "You two look great out there. Good couple."

Miss Ginny said, "Thank you."

Ashley patted J.W.'s knee. "Don't let him get away."

Miss Ginny just smiled at J.W. "I won't." She watched Ashley walk away, then looked at J.W. "You have quite a little fan club in here."

"What?" he said. "I just party here."

She rolled her eyes. "Okay, if that's what you think."

"Besides, you got them all beat, hands down."

She looked at him. "Good answer, big boy."

Soon, it was last call. Time to go.

"Okay, baby, my place."

They went a few doors down to Maryjane's Pizza. It was really good, and they got a large supreme, to go. When it was ready, they called J.W., and he walked in to get it.

"Okay. We have food, beer. We are good to go," Miss Ginny said. "And Tarantula tequila." She had it put in the limo just for him.

On the way home, they had shots and a beer. One just can't beat a limo for barhopping. As they got to the house, J.W. said, "Got the pizza."

She said, "Okay, I got two beers."

They got out of the car. The driver got a bag out of the trunk and gave it to Miss Ginny. J.W. unlocked the front door. Rocky was there to meet them.

"Okay, down, boy." J.W. turned off the alarm and closed and locked the door.

They sat down at the table to eat the pizza.

She said, "I need to change."

"Okay. You know where things are."

He had a thought. He went out on the back porch, turned on the Christmas lights, and uncovered the hot tub.

She came out of the bathroom in shorts and a T-shirt.

J.W. said, "I have an idea. Here's a robe. Let's sit in the hot tub."

"Great idea."

J.W. got undressed and went out. She had the pizza on the table next to the hot tub and a bucket full of beer next to the pizza. She's good. He was about to climb in when there was a knock at the door and flashing lights outside.

J.W. answered it in his robe. His best friend, Mike Pantuso, was at the door. "You got to come with me."

"Okay, step inside."

"Some guy filed assault charges."

"Okay, let me get dressed."

About that time, Miss Ginny came in. "Is there something wrong?"

"Your brother filed charges, so I have to see the night judge," J.W. said. He had to get dressed."

She went to change.

Mike said, "Where did you meet her? She's gorgeous."

J.W. said, "I know, and your timing sucks. We were about to get in the hot tub."

"Sorry, brother, can you put the cover back on and turn it off? There's pizza." As he walked out, J.W. heard him say, "Ha, it's Maryjane's Pizza, still hot."

She came out, dressed in jeans and a T-shirt. J.W. went in, put on a pair of shorts and an Old Guard T-shirt. As he came out, Mike was stuffing his face with pizza.

"Ha, give me a slice."

Miss Ginny called her driver and her lawyer to meet them there.

They got into the squad car. J.W. was eating pizza, and Miss Ginny was getting mad at her brother.

Mike was telling jokes. "Did you hear that 95 percent of Harleys are still on the road and the other 5 percent made it home?"

"Yeah, you're funny. Last I checked, I had to tow your Kawasaki home."

"Ha ha ha, very funny."

J.W. thought it was. They need to go on a long ride again.

"We sure do."

Miss Ginny said, "Aren't you guys worried?"

They both said, "No."

"So when do you want to go? After Sparks America bike rally?"

"Sounds good. We can ride home to San Diego in August."

"That sounds great."
"Okay, we are here. Are you ready?"
Miss Ginny said, "No."
They laughed.

CHAPTER 13

A Day in Court

Sunday morning

They got out of the car. All the other cops wanted to know why J.W. was not in cuffs.

Mike just said, "He's my prisoner, and I do what I want. Next question?"

All the officers just walked away.

Miss Ginny said, "He's like you, J.W."

They laughed again.

The three of them walked into the court. Her brother was there with a large black eye and a stupid look on his face.

J.W. said, "Ha, Mike, he thinks he will win."

Mike and J.W. laughed again.

As they were standing there, a man walked in. It was Miss Ginny's lawyer. She ran over to him in a panic. She talked to him and pointed at J.W.

Mike said, "She thinks you need a lawyer."

J.W. replied, "Apparently."

A man with a small case came in and sat down. Mike and J.W. started to talk about old times in Laredo, Texas.

The judge came in. He sat down, looked at the courtroom, and saw J.W. "Hi, Mr. Santee, how are you these days?"

J.W. replied, "Just fine, Robert. Been out to the range lately?"

"No, been on nights."

"I know how that feels."

About that time, Mark, Miss Ginny's brother, said, "Can we get started?"

The judge looked at him. "You are Michael Brown the Third? Okay, you're the a——hole with no respect for the court?"

J.W. looked at Mike. Mike just rolled his eyes and smiled.

The judge said, "Bailiff, read the charges."

"The charges are assault and battery."

"Now how do you plead?"

J.W. said, "Not guilty."

About that time, Miss Ginny's lawyer told the judge he was there to defend J.W.

The judge looked at him. "Wait, are you new, son?"

The lawyer said, "No, Your Honor. I've been a lawyer for twenty years."

The judge laughed. "No, defending Mr. Santee."

"Yes, sir, first time."

The judge looked at J.W. "Why?"

"I had no idea," J.W. said. "This is my girlfriend's lawyer. Apparently, she thinks I need one."

The judge broke out in laughter. "Sorry, what? You have a girlfriend?"

Miss Ginny said, "Yes, me."

The judge turned his sights on her. "Well, ain't you something." She said, "Thank you."

"All right," the judge said. "Back to the case. Any witnesses?"

Mark said, "My two bodyguards."

The judge said, "Do you pay these men?"

"Well, yes."

"Disqualified. Anyone else?"

"None, Your Honor."

Miss Ginny and Richard.

"Okay, who's first? Richard? Please enter the witness-box."

He was sworn in.

J.W. questioned him. "Do I pay you?"

"No, sir."

"What did you see?"

Richard said, "Mr. Brown grabbed Miss Ginny's arm and jerked her to him. Mr. Santee told him to remove his hands from Miss Ginny's arm. Mr. Brown refused to. So Mr. Santee removed his hand from Miss Ginny for him and restrained him. Mr. Santee let him go, and Mr. Brown moved in a threatening manner towards Miss Ginny. Mr. Santee eliminated the threat."

The judge asked Miss Ginny, "Is that how it went?"

She said, "Yes."

Mark's lawyer said, "Objection."

The judge looked at him. "To what?"

The lawyer said, "Not sure."

About that time, the man with the little case stood up and walked to the bench and handed the judge a piece of paper.

The judge read it. He looked back at the Brown's table. "As much as I'd like to see you prove this. But case dismissed."

Mark yelled at the judge, "What the hell? Did he pay you off?"

The judge slammed his gavel down. "Contempt of court. Three days in jail. Mr. Santee, you are free to go."

They watched Mark be put in cuffs and dragged away in his $3,000 suit.

Mike and J.W. were chatting.

"Do you think?" J.W. asked. "Should I ask the judge to let him out?"

Mike said, "You could, but it won't help. He accused the judge of taking a bribe, and that just pissed him off. I think he was being nice with three days for you. The last guy got thirty days."

J.W. said, "Well, I will have to take the judge out drinking again as a thank-you."

They laughed again.

Miss Ginny was in front of them, and turned around. "You two are terrible." She smiled. "He should have gotten more. My brother is an a———hole. Wait till my dad hears about this. I don't know if he will be mad or laugh." She turned to Richard. "You were great in there."

Her lawyer walked up to the three of them. "Miss Ginny, will there be anything else?"

"After all, you didn't really do anything," she said. "That's all right."

He turned to J.W. "What, may I ask, was on the paper?"

"The man gave the judge a release from the state department."

"How did you get one so fast?"

J.W. said, "I have a stack of them. All the little man has to do is put a date on it, notarize it, and bring it to the courtroom, and I go home. The man works for the state department here in Tulsa."

Miss Ginny's lawyer asked, "What did you do to get that kind of treatment?"

J.W. said, "I did a few jobs for the government, and this is what I wanted for payment."

On the way home, Mike said, "Ya, we was down in San Antonio and got picked up after a fight in a bar. The cops wanted to teach us a lesson and threw us in the cell with a motorcycle gang. When the cops came to get us, after they ran our IDs, they came to the cell, and we were at the table playing cards. The bikers were all around us out cold! So they let us go. The cops gave us a ride to our hotel. We saw that gang the next day. They were very nice and polite, so we invited them to lunch. Suddenly, they had appointments and had to go."

Mike dropped them off at J.W.'s place. It was dawn, and they were tired. They got undressed and went straight to bed.

"Good thing I'm off tonight," J.W. said.

The two of them climbed into bed, with her long red hair in J.W.'s hands. He ran his fingers through it. They drifted off to sleep.

About 4:00 a.m., J.W. woke up to a ninety-one-pound dog whining at J.W. He wanted out. J.W. went to get up, and there was no one in the bed with him.

He heard the water turn on in the shower. *Well, that explains that.*

J.W. popped his head in. "Do you want to sit in the hot tub first?"

She smiled. "That's a wonderful idea. Have some coffee."

"You bet. I will get it started."

J.W. put his robe on and left one for her on the door. He let Rocky out.

He made the coffee okay and turned the On button. "Okay, coffee's started."

He looked at the doorway. A long and very sexy leg came around the doorframe. Then she peeked around the doorframe.

"What a leg," J.W. said.

She came around the doorway with her hair across her shoulders. She was gorgeous.

J.W. said, "Coffee's almost ready."

He toasted some bagels with cream cheese, got two mugs from the cabinet. He would fill those. "And if you will get that plate, we can go out to the tub."

She set them on the table.

As soon as Rocky saw her, he came running to see her.

"He sure likes you."

She slyly said, "Is he the only one?"

So being the smart-ass J.W. is, he said, "For now."

She spanked J.W. on his ass.

They talked about her family, why her brother was such a d——ck and how she turned out so sweet. As they sat in the hot tub, J.W. was against the wall, with her in front of him leaning against him. He played with her breast. She would run her hand down the outside of his leg.

He began to get hard. She climbed onto him, and they were splashing water out of the tub. After she came, she turned and leaned over the edge of the hot tub. He came in behind her. They made waves; water was coming out of the hot tub. She was beautiful from behind. He kept going. She curved her back so she could kiss him. As he came, she did too. They both collapsed back into the water, but there was a lot less now.

They got out. J.W. helped her with her robe; he got his on. He got the empty coffee mugs and the plate and went in and put them on the counter. He heard the shower water start, so he let Rocky in the house. He dropped his robe onto the bathroom floor and climbed in with her. They soaped each other up and washed her hair and all the fun parts. They got out; her phone rang.

She went to get it and dried off as she was talking. J.W. took a towel and dried her off as she talked to her father. He heard her say, "We would love to come. Goodbye."

She looked at J.W. "do you know how hard it is to talk on the phone as you rub a towel all over my nude body?" She threw a pillow at him. "My father has invited us to dinner tonight."

J.W. asked, "What do I have to wear, a suit?"

She rolled her eyes at him. "No, just look nice, okay?"

"Okay, but I'm not happy about this. What time?"

"Eight p.m."

J.W. said, "I will come get you, okay?"

"Sure."

Her car pulled up out front. She got dressed and went out the door.

What about that? No kiss goodbye? Well, it's 6:30. I better get ready.

CHAPTER 14

Meeting Her Parents

Sunday night

After he showered and shaved, J.W. pulled out a pink shirt and black pants with black boots. He looked into the mirror; there was something missing. He grabbed a lavender tie; that did it. He put his shoulder gun holster on, wiped down his .45-70, loaded it, and put it in.

J.W. slipped on his jean jacket. He looked again. Well, that should do it; just enough style and still more him. He put on his old gray hat that has sweat stains in it, just to let her know he works for a living. He turned to Rocky. "So what do you think?"

He started barking at J.W.

"Ooh, you want to play, do ya? Well, come on outside. There, big boy."

They played his favorite game, and he was having fun. There was a knock at the door. It was Richard.

J.W. said, "Ha. Come on in."

Richard asked if J.W. was okay.

"Yeah, why?" J.W. replied.

"It sounded like he was tearing you up."

"We were just playing."

Rocky was standing there, waiting to play some more.

J.W. had to tell him, "Okay, Rocky, go lie down." These were the code words for him to know he was back on duty. He went and looked out the back door, then came back and laid down.

"Okay, he's ready. Are you, Richard?"

J.W. closed the front door and set the alarm, and they both left the house. With his hat in his hand, J.W. stepped into the car. Richard joined him.

"So tell me about Miss Ginny's dad."

"Well, he's a lot like you: ex-military, a man who gets what he wants most of the time. I figure you two will be best friends or butt heads a lot."

"Well, thanks for the encouragement."

Richard just smiled. "Anytime."

They rode back to Miss Ginny's place to get her. Of course, she wasn't ready.

J.W. said, "What woman is?"

They sat in the car waiting. J.W. had a beer. She finally came out, and it was well worth the wait. She looked wonderful in a pink dress and with her red hair down. She was lovely. She stepped into the car and kissed J.W.

"What was that for?"

She smiled. "For good luck."

The car pulled away.

"So where does your dad live?"

"Over by swan lake."

"Oh, down by the little houses?"

They all laughed.

They finally arrived. It looked smaller than Miss Ginny's place, but not small at all. As they pulled up, a man opened the door of the car and helped Miss Ginny out. As J.W. stepped out, Richard suggested he leave his jacket, gun, and holster here; Richard would watch them. J.W. had learned to trust Richard. He hasn't failed him yet.

J.W. walked with Miss Ginny on his arm to the front door; it opened just as they got to it. There was a lady in a long dress who looked like she just stepped out of a fashion magazine. She was in her late sixties but looked great. She hugged Miss Ginny. She was all smiles until she looked at J.W. Then her nose went up, and her face went blank.

Miss Ginny turned to J.W. "This is J.W. Santee, my boyfriend." She looked J.W. up and down.

He kept thinking, *Where's my gun?* He looked back at the car. It had pulled away.

Smart boys.

They walked in. Her mother separated them: Miss Ginny in front, then she and J.W. in the rear.

Well, he could see this is going to be a lot of fun.

They walked in. There was an old man in his seventies.

J.W. was thinking, *Late seventies.* The man was trying to move a table down a hallway by himself. J.W. saw that and went over to help. "Would you like a hand with this?"

The older gentleman said, "Sure, young fella. You get one end, and I will get the other."

They carried it down the hall.

He could hear her mother saying, "Why would you be with someone so beneath you?"

Miss Ginny said, "Because he makes me happy, and that ain't easy."

J.W. and the older man came into the room he wanted to put the table in. They had to take it in on its side.

They turned with him in a mirror image. As they lifted the table, he went though at an angle, then evened out, then angled so J.W. can get the legs in. After they got it in, they set it flat again and against a wall.

He looked at J.W. "Have you moved furniture before?"

"A few times, and a whole summer in high school."

"Well, at least you're not worthless, like some of the men she's brought around. Never worked a day in their lives."

J.W. put his hand out. The man looked a little surprised in his overalls.

He took J.W.'s hand and said, "Augusta Brown. I'm Miss Ginny's dad."

Now it was J.W.'s turn to look surprised. "You're not what I expected."

He smiled. "I never am. I tried to get some info on you, but there's not much out there."

"There's a reason for that."

Miss Ginny's dad looked at J.W. "Well, there's nothing bad, so I will go with that. I'm going to have a shot and a beer. Care to join me?"

J.W. said, "Sure. I don't have to work tonight, and I have a driver. Why not?"

They both walked to a room and then into a kitchen, where he walked up to the fridge, opened the freezer, and pulled out a bottle of Tarantula tequila. Then he went to the fridge and got two George Killian beers.

J.W. thought, *He's a man I can get along with.*

J.W. said, "I will get the glasses if you would tell me where they are."

He nodded to a cabinet, and J.W. pulled out three shot glasses. He put the three onto the table.

Augusta looked at J.W. "Army man?"

"Yes. Oh, I guess you would know that."

"Nope, not in the reports."

"How would you know?"

Three shots, only two people. Lost brothers. He pulled a Seals shot glass with bourbon in it.

J.W. thought, *He did this years ago.*

"Good idea."

J.W. was pouring the two shots. Miss Ginny came in without her mother, grabbed one shot, and downed it. J.W. pulled the other shot glass around, filled it, and refilled Miss Ginny's glass. They toasted to the lost men of battle. Her father, as they were done, reached into the fridge for one more beer.

As the three of them sat talking, her mother came in and had a hissy fit. "Drinking in the middle of the day? What has gotten into you three?"

Her dad held his hand up. "For one thing, it's 8:30 p.m. at night. Also, I'm seventy-seven years old, and I will do what I want. My friend J.W. is forty-nine years old and does what he wants, and my little girl is—"

Miss Ginny stopped him right there. "Okay, Dad, Mom knows she's wrong. Sit down, Mom, and have a beer."

Her dad pulled four more out. The four of them sat talking without airs. Just four nice people having dinner. Miss Ginny told them about how J.W. took her to the gun range, how much fun she had, and off-roading in the jeep. J.W. was glad she left a few parts out.

Her dad said, "That sounds like fun. Have to try that some time."

J.W. said, "You're always welcome. I'm going again next Saturday. The jeep holds four."

After a while, a lady came in and asked if they were going to eat dinner.

Miss Ginny's mom, Virginia, said, "I forgot all about dinner."

J.W. looked around. "Where did they cook it?"

"In the main kitchen," Miss Ginny's father said. "This one's just for us. My wife's a really good cook. Sometimes I want her cooking. This is where she cooks and where I keep my beer."

J.W. tipped his bottle to him. He drank the same thing.

"Ask Miss Ginny." He looked at her.

She said, "Ever since the first time I met him and Tarantula tequila. It's his favorite."

They all walked into the other room to eat. J.W. ran into one of his favorite waitresses, Gloria. She used to work at the Freeway Café. Good food. She walked over to J.W. with a big hug.

He asked her, "How are you? I missed you at the Freeway. It's not the same without you there."

She said, "Mr. Brown offered me a job here for twice the pay. He didn't have to ask twice. I've been here ever since."

"Well, it's good to see you."

They all sat down. There was steak any way one wanted it, roast beef, mashed potatoes, corn on the cob, broccoli, and brussels sprouts—J.W.'s favorite. They had dinner. J.W. had a rib eye, medium rare, cooked to perfection. Everything was great.

After dinner, they sat out on the pool area and had coffee. It was a great night.

It was getting close to 1:30 a.m.

J.W. said, "Don't want to be rude, but I have a dog at home that probably needs out soon."

Augusta said, "Don't be a stranger."

J.W. said, "I can't. We are going four-wheeling on Saturday."

They walked to the front door, said their goodbyes, and walked down to the car. Richard met them.

He asked, "How did you like the old man?"

"Hell, he is great. They are going four-wheeling next Saturday."

They all got in the car and headed to J.W.'s house.

CHAPTER 15

Two Dead Bodies

Monday

As they rode back to J.W.'s house, they talked about the off-roading they will do on Saturday and what they should pack to eat out there.

They came around the corner to J.W.'s street. They could see cop cars with their lights on. As they went down the street, J.W. could see they were at his house. He quickly grabbed his phone. It was off. "Richard, did you turn off my phone? It was in my jacket."

He said, "No."

They pulled up. J.W. stepped out. Some cop told him he couldn't go up there. J.W. pushed past him.

Mike saw J.W. "It's your dog, Rocky. He won't let us near the body."

J.W. said, "Body? What body?"

As they came around the side of the house, they saw there were three cops with guns out and Rocky guarding a body up against his gate. As soon as J.W. saw Rocky, J.W. said, "Sit." Rocky did.

Mike told the cops to put their guns away. They "weren't too sure," one of them said.

He walked past J.W. "That dog is a killer and should be put down."

J.W. turned to him. "That dog is one of the best guard dogs in the world, and he's doing what he was trained to do. Rock, heel."

Rocky walked over to J.W. and sat next to his foot.

Mike said, "Can you let me in the house?"

"Sure, Mike. Rocky, walk." J.W. walked, and Rocky walked with him like they were at a dog show. When Rocky moved, about six cops backed up.

Mike said, "No food or water for him. He's evidence."

They walked around to the front porch. Richard and Miss Ginny were standing on the porch. Miss Ginny reached down to pet Rocky, but Richard pulled her back. "He's evidence now."

J.W. unlocked the front door; the alarm was still going off. He stepped inside, went to the keypad, punched in the code, and let the keypad scan his left thumb. After that, the alarm stopped, and they could hear all the cops trampling J.W.'s yard to death.

From his view, J.W. could see the back door. The glass was busted out. Rocky was sitting next to Miss Ginny. J.W. told him, "Sit. Stay."

He told Miss Ginny, "No patting the top of his head."

Once she did, and he looked at her.

J.W. said, "On guard."

Rocky stood up, walked around Miss Ginny, and sat on the other side of her. She was by the wall, and Rocky was between her and everyone else.

Now she's safe, and he's busy. J.W. made a jump into the kitchen and flipped on an overhead light.

Mike stood in the dining area. "Well, it looks like they broke the bottom glass panel out and stepped in. By that boot print. That's where Rocky got them. He was in here."

"How can you tell that? Do you see where the glass is moved in? These four lines, Rocky's legs sliding, they slide away from the kitchen. What about that pool of blood? It's on both sides of the boot print. Rocky got that leg good."

Mike moved into the kitchen, grabbed a dish towel, and unlocked the back door. He stepped onto the doorway. He saw a bigger pool of blood on the back porch, but the spray was in a circular pattern.

"He must have been trying to fight off Rocky," Mike said. "Good luck with that."

He grinned as they made their way following the blood trail. It went to the back to the exit door. They stepped out into the yard. About five feet from the porch steps was another body, but this one had a bullet hole in his forehead.

"Well, Rocky didn't do that."

The victim had his hair cut short and was wearing a wife-beater shirt. He had on pants that the kids wear around their butts. J.W. thought it was a stupid way to wear pants with your ass hanging out, but this young man's pants were around his ankles for some reason.

J.W. said, "Well, there's where they got into my backyard."

They could see where they kicked out some of the fence. As they walked over, they saw a .38 revolver lying in the grass by the fence.

Mike looked through the hole. There was a 10 ten-sledgehammer and J.W.'s neighbor's gate off its hinges, a trail of blood out the gate. J.W. unlocked the gate so they could collect the bodies. The one by the gate had a bad dog bite on his right leg and two bullet wounds: one in his thigh and one in the back of his head.

"Well, Rocky didn't do that either."

The cops took over. J.W. went back into the house, picked up Rocky's food and water buckets, placed them onto the counter, and then told Rocky, "Okay, off duty."

Rocky then came over and sat in front of J.W.

The CSI guys came in. At first, Rocky turned on them. J.W. said, "It's okay," and Rocky was all wiggles then calmed down, and the CSI guys took dental swabs. When they were through with Rocky, they moved into the dining area.

J.W. said to Miss Ginny, "Maybe we should stay at your place for the night. Let me grab a few things. But first, let me check out Rocky."

He looked at all four paws and worked his way over him. "He's fine. Good boy. Do you want to go?" Rocky started wiggling all over the place.

J.W. walked into the bedroom and got some fresh clothing and the remote for the alarm. He walked out with a gym bag in his hand.

Mike walked in and said, "You might—" He stopped. He looked at the bag in J.W.'s hand. "Oh, I guess you know."

J.W. tossed him the fob to the alarm. "When they are done, lock it up and set the alarm. That's the remote to it. Oh, yeah." J.W. stepped back into the bedroom and got his phone charger and shampoo for Rocky. "Okay, we can go now."

They all walked out to the car. He put Rocky and Miss Ginny in the car. He remembered food. He walked back in, got the two buckets, poured out the water, put the food bucket into it, and walked back out to the car.

As they pulled out, Miss Ginny asked, "Do you always have this kind of thing happen in your neighborhood?"

"No. Most people know better, and there's just not a lot of crime in this area, so I'm not sure what's up. But they can't do it again."

As they got to Miss Ginny's place, J.W. let Rocky out to run and get rid of any frustrations from the night. He got all his things together, including his gun and coat.

They walked up to the door. J.W. called, "Rocky, come." He was there, panting but okay.

As they got to Miss Ginny's room, J.W. took off Rocky's body harness and walked him into the bathroom. He got two towels out J.W. brought from home. He got undressed, and Rocky and J.W. got into the shower. J.W. washed Rocky as well as himself. When they were done, J.W. stepped out and dried off.

He let Rocky out; it was his favorite part, drying him off. When they were done, J.W. let Rocky out, and Miss Ginny watched him bounce and wiggle all over the place. Her little dog was chasing after him.

J.W. sat down on the bed. He could feel the day weigh heavy on his shoulders. Miss Ginny moved to the top of the bed and told him to come lie in her arms. He did, and before he knew it, J.W. was sound asleep.

Rocky laid down, and her dog laid down with him. Miss Ginny slipped out of bed, covered J.W. up, and climbed in with him. With her arms around him, they fell asleep.

CHAPTER 16

Repairing the Damage

Monday noon

J.W. awoke to the smell of coffee in the air. About that time, Miss Ginny came through the door with a tray of food and coffee, and set them on the table in her room with two chairs. She saw J.W. and smiled, and she asked what he was going to do with that gun.

That was when he realized he had it in his hand, holding it straight up. He looked around and remembered where he was. Just as he remembered, she said, "You sure were tired last night, and you must have had some bad dreams, because you twitched all night until I wrapped my arms around you. Then you calmed down a bit. Are you going to put the gun down?"

He was still holding the gun. He slid it into its holster. She poured him some coffee and made a plate of food.

He climbed out of bed. Rocky was chewing on a bone.

"Where did he get that?"

"The cook saved it for him. You know, they're becoming friends."

Rocky liked the bone. Her dog tried to chew on it and lost interest, so Rocky took over.

"He's been busy all morning," she said. "So come, eat. You got work today."

"That's right. What time is it?"

"Just about twelve o'clock. We got home about three, and after you washed Rocky and got into bed, it was about 4 a.m. You slept about ten hours. You were wiped out, so come, eat something."

He put the new robe on. It fit much better than the last one.

"Where did you get this robe? It fits."

She asked why. Because he wanted to get a few for the house.

"Oh, the house!" J.W. had to fix the fence and back door.

She said, "You're not thinking straight. Get over here and sit."

He did. She gave him coffee, eggs, and hash browns with everything, bagels with pineapple cream cheese. It was all great.

She said, "Don't worry about your place. Richard went over with a work crew this morning and fixed the fence. Your friend Mike went with them to release the property so they could get to work. Mike called me half an hour ago and said they were all done with the back door, and they put a doggy door in for Rocky. He has a thing you put on his collar, and only he can come through that door. They had to get some wood to fix the fence. That's where they are."

"What about the blood everywhere?"

"Mike called one of those teams that clean up stuff like that, and they did it as a favor to Mike. They owed him one or something."

"Okay. How much is this going to cost me?" J.W. asked.

She looked at him all sweet, with bows in her hair, and said, "Nothing. They were on my work crew for the property. They were in-between jobs."

She was paying them to sit around, anyway. Miss Ginny sent them over. The doggy door had been in the storage room, waiting. Miss Ginny was getting a dog. They thought it would be one like Rocky, not like what she got. So at least it was being used.

J.W. just looked at her. He only had two things to say: "I thank you very much. How much coffee have you had this morning? You're bouncing off the walls."

She smiled even bigger. She walked over and kissed him. She was up all night worrying about J.W. and who was after him. He pulled her into his lap and kissed her again.

Then he said, "So what do you say we eat? I'm suddenly hungry."

She sat down. J.W. drank some coffee. The food was great. He was hungrier than he thought. After that, J.W. got dressed, and they walked outside with the dogs. As they ran in the warm sunlight, the two of them talked, and they walked around front just as the guys came back.

Mike walked up and said, "Here's your alarm fob and this strip to go in to Rocky's collar. The place looks great, like nothing ever happened."

J.W. shook his hand. "Thank you, Mike."

"He was trying to call you this morning, but your phone was off," Miss Ginny said.

"Forgot to plug it in last night."

Michelle came out with J.W.'s phone. She walked over to him. "Here's your phone, all charged up."

"Well, thank you very much," J.W. said.

Mike laughed. "It seems like you're having a great day. You think of something, and it appears! Sweet, brother. Sweet." He walked off, laughing.

Okay, now all J.W. needed was a ride to his place so he can put a work shirt on and drive to work.

Miss Ginny said, "You can take one of the cars in the garage."

But how will he get it back here?

"That's easy. When you come back tonight."

Mike said, "That's a good idea, until I can get IDs on those two bodies."

"Okay. Come on, Mike, let's look in the garage."

They walked through the main door. There were twenty-seven cars in there.

Mike looked at J.W. "Well, what do you want to drive?"

J.W. said, "It's more like what will I fit in."

Well, the sports cars were out.

"You'd have to grease me up to get in!" J.W. exclaimed.

They both laughed.

"The limos are out. Now we are down to three cars: a Ford bronco 1977 model, a security guard's car with 'Security' down the side, and a 1974 Chevy Caprice convertible."

"Big car." Mike looked at J.W.

"Yep" was all he had to say.

When J.W. pulled out of the garage, Miss Ginny was reaching over to Richard as he handed her money.

"Okay, betting on what he would pick?"

Richard said, "She said you would drive out in that, and I said you wouldn't. So we bet, and out of all those cars, she was right."

Mike got out. She was starting to know J.W.'s taste. He liked that.

She smiled. "Besides, it's the one my dad got for me in high school, so the odds were in my favor."

J.W. said, "Well, I got to get to work. Be back later."

He called Rocky, who came running across the grass, her little dog way behind. Mike held the door, and Rocky jumped into the back seat. Michelle put his dog food and water bucket in the back floorboard. J.W. put the car into gear, and he was off to his house.

J.W. pulled up into the drive.

His neighbor said, "Nice car."

"It's not mine, but it's fun to drive."

They went inside. He looked at the back door. "Nice work."

They put the doggy door on one side and glass on the other. "Nice job."

He remembered about that piece for Rocky's collar, so he reached down and pulled off his collar and looked at it. He walked over to a drawer and pulled out two small wire zip ties and added the door fob to Rocky's collar. He put it back on Rocky.

J.W. walked out but left Rocky inside. As he got closer, he could move the doggy door so he could see. J.W. turned to check the fence and the shop. They were fine. J.W. turned. Rocky was there, so he told him, "Good boy." Then J.W. went back inside and got work keys and a shirt. Rocky was there in the living room, so J.W. set the alarm and was off to work. It was a nice day, and the top down made it perfect.

He got to work and clocked in. J.W. let things spin in his mind. He worked in the DBCS area. He called it "think mode." J.W. figured there was nothing he can do yet. He needed more info.

Later, when he got off, J.W. stopped by the Harvard to have a beer and a shot. As he sat there, Ashley, the waitress with the tattoos, sat next to him. "Everything all right? You look down."

"No, just thinking."

Mike walked in. "J.W., I need to talk to you."

"What's up, Mike?"

"Those guys killed in your yard."

Ashley perked up. "Nothing going on, huh?" She walked away.

Mike said, "A couple punks from a local street gang, the Dogs."

"Yeah, I know a few of them."

Mike and J.W. both looked at Ashley.

J.W. asked, "How can I talk to one of the leaders?"

She laughed. "You know him. Patrick, come over here."

Patrick came over.

"Are you a member of the Dog's gang?" J.W. asked.

He moved in closer. "Not so loud. One of the locals, why?"

"Well, two of your members were found dead outside my house."

Patrick said, "What? I put your house and block off limits because of that dog of yours. He's almost as mean as you, but he's not as kind."

Mike said, "You ain't kidding there."

Patrick looked at Mike.

J.W. said, "He's a cop. Not right now. He's my friend, same as you. Why was they there? Breaking into my place?"

"I have no idea, but, for you, I will find out. Give me a day or two." Patrick looked at Mike. "When can we have our friends back?"

Mike said, "I will check on them, but a funeral home has to get the bodies. It's the law."

Patrick said, "I can take care of that."

Mike smiled. "I will find out."

Patrick walked over to his buddies. He said something, and all five guys left in a hurry. Patrick walked up to pay their bill. J. W told Ashley it was on him. Patrick tipped his head and walked out.

"Mike, are you off duty?"

He said, "Ya, why?"

J.W. looked at Ashley bringing two rounds. Mike and J.W. toasted. Ashley walked up with a shot on her tray. She squeezed in between them so the camera couldn't see her. They toasted, all three of them.

"To friends."

Ashley stole a swig off J.W.'s beer. He didn't care. "You better put that shot on my tab and bring us some more."

As the two of them drank a few and thought things through, one of Patrick's boys came in and asked J.W. for his phone number for Patrick. J.W. gave him his card—his US veterans club card. He looked as the man's eyes got large, and his demeanor changed.

"Thank you, sir." He walked out backward.

Mike said, "What was that all about?"

J.W. said, "I gave him my club card. He knows it's a motorcycle club."

Mike said, "It's a street rod club too."

"I know, but most people see what they want to see. Most street gangs fear bike clubs. They are just the next step in the food chain. Most 1 percent come from street gangs. Let's go home, okay?"

"If it's all right, I will borrow your guest room."

"Why not? You still have a change of clothing in there, I think."

Mike usually stayed at J.W.'s place if he's worked too many hours or they have been out drinking.

He followed J.W. It was the only time J.W. felt safe with a cop behind him. They got to the house, and it was all lit up.

J.W. pulled up to the back gate, with Mike behind him. They went into the house and through to the backyard. J.W. unlocked the back gate and pushed it open.

As he started to pull in, something caught his headlights. Rocky had something pinned in the back corner of the yard.

J.W. pulled up to the shop door. Mike pulled in and saw the same thing J.W. did.

Mike yelled out, "Is he dead?"

"No," J.W. said.

Mike said, "Hang on, I will get a couple of cars here ASAP."

As Rocky held the kid, a shot rang out and hit Mike's back window. Mike bailed out. Behind the house, two more shots hit just above the kid. J.W. yelled at him, "Lie flat!"

He did.

J.W. yelled at Rocky, "Play dead!"

The dog laid down flat.

J.W. said, "Stay."

He went around the house to see where the shots were coming from. As Mike distracted the shooter, the shooter moved his rifle barrel. The light flashed off it, and J.W. could see his hand. J.W. took out his .45-70 and laid it on the fence for support. He fired and knocked the rifle out of the shooter's hands. He thought he had hit him in the hand.

J.W. came running around the house. The kid was starting to move.

J.W. yelled, "Rocky, on guard!"

He popped up, and the kid sat back down.

"Mike, he's on the roof across the street with a rifle."

He rounded the house. J.W. could hear tires squealing.

He ran on. J.W. pointed at the rifle and, Mike stopped as three cop cars came around to J.W.'s street from the other end, letting the shooter get away.

"Damn!"

Mike asked, "He got away. Did you see the car?"

J.W. said, "No, it was gone. We still got the kid and the rifle. It's a good start."

The rifle and the kid were taken into custody. J.W. put Miss Ginny's car in the shop, and Mike's car was now evidence. They called it a night.

They sat on the back porch, having a cold one. J.W. called Miss Ginny. "I won't be there tonight."

She was glad they were all right. They had another beer, with Rocky asleep at J.W.'s feet. The weight of the day was closing in on them.

They finished their beers and went inside. J.W. set the timer on the coffee maker so Mike could have coffee in the morning. Mike set his phone's alarm. There was a power plug in the guest room he used.

J.W. went to bed. Rocky was already taking up most of the bed, but when J.W. sat down to take his boots off, he moved over. He set the alarm for 9:00 a.m. and remembered he hadn't set the house alarm yet. He got up and turned it on. He laid down and heard the alarm say, "Set for stay."

J.W. dozed off. He slept well.

As he got up, Mike was making more coffee.

J.W. asked, "What are you doing here?"

CHAPTER 17

The Man in the Blue Chevy

Tuesday morning

Mike said, "Looking at the crime scene. You were out of it this morning. So I let you sleep. Besides, I know all the codes here anyway. By the way, it looks like you hit him last night with that cannon you carry around. Made a mess of that rifle. It's bent, the barrel. That thing's a beast."

J.W. said, "But it did the job."

Mike poured them both a cup. They talked about what all they had found. There was a blood trail out back of the empty house. They had tire tracks and blood and a weapon. Now if they just had this guy.

"What about the kid?"

Mike said, "He's from a gang from across town. He said a guy paid him five large to break in and put all over the house out these listening devices."

"I wonder why," J.W. said. "Real spooks. Couldn't get in to plant anything. So this kid didn't have a chance."

"Nope. Are you hungry?"

"Why, do you want me to make you breakfast?"

"No, I was going to take you to Freeways. I'm buying."

J.W. said, "That sounds good." He got dressed.

They went outside and remembered Mike's car was taken for evidence.

J.W. said, "Okay, we can take the jeep. It's been a while, and I need to get gas in it."

They climbed in. It was parked under the overhang. There was something under J.W.'s feet.

Mike said, "Don't move."

J.W. didn't. Mike went out across the street to get the team.

They came over and looked at what J.W. had stepped on. He felt around it to see if it was a bomb or not

Mike said, "Lift your leg slowly."

J.W. did. He took the bag out of the jeep and placed it in the center of the yard.

Mike unzipped the bag. "It's a cosmetic bag."

They all could breathe again.

J.W. called Miss Ginny. "Are you missing a cosmetic bag?"

She said, "Yes, did you find it?"

"Yes, I did. I will bring it out tonight."

"Thank you, sweetheart." She hung up.

J.W. put the bag on the back porch. He jumped into the jeep and fired it up. Mike waited for him to pull through the gate, then locked the house, set the alarm, and came out. As he was just about to jump into the jeep, one of the forensics team called him over. They talked, and he walked over.

Mike asked, "Are you still wearing the boots you had on last night?"

"Yes," J.W. said.

"Go make an impression for him so he can know which ones are yours."

"Okay." J.W. put the jeep in neutral and walked over. "Where do you want my footprints?"

"Here, next to Detective Pantuso's."

He stepped on the spot he wanted and stepped out. "Will that do?"

"That's perfect," he said. "Hey, are you going to Freeways?"

"Yes, we are."

"Call me before you leave. Mike's got my number."

Mike said, "Sure. Do you want biscuits and gravy?"

The forensics man did a thumbs-up gesture, as J.W. climbed back into the jeep. He took off.

Mike grabbed the Jesus bar. "You in some kind of hurry?"

"Yes, before something else happens."

"Why didn't we take the Chevy Miss Ginny loaned you?"

J.W. said, "I will, when they get back." He put tape on the door's hood and trunk lid so he would know if anyone touched it today, and anyone watching him would know he rarely drives the jeep.

J.W. said, "I turned on all the cameras today so we can watch at Freeways."

Mike said, "You never cease to surprise me."

They got to the diner. J.W. set up the iPad so he could see all six camera shots. Someone pulled up across the street. It was a dark-blue Chevy. It was that car J.W. had seen all over town. The driver had sandy-blond hair, was about 160 pounds and five feet eight to six feet. He had hired a gang banger to stab J.W. a week or two ago. He was the one J.W. shot and hit his gun to his face.

J.W. had no idea what he wanted with him.

Mike's phone rang. It was the guys from the forensic team. "There's a guy just watching the house. What do you want us to do?"

Mike said, "Try to get a plate number."

Just about that time, the guy on the camera was looking the way of the forensics team.

"Mike, he sees them. Are they armed?"

The guys pull their guns. The guy in the car put the car in reverse and started moving backward. The forensics team moved forward. He hit the gas, and halfway down the street, the guy in the Chevy wiped the steering wheel. The car spun in the opposite direction. The guy shifted to drive and left the area.

Mike asked, "J.W., do you have that recorded?"

"Yes, at an offsite area."

"Great!"

J.W. said, "I will email you the file now."

"I have some news," Mike said.

Their food came.

"The two guys found at your house, according to what I can piece together from all the reports, the one found out by the gate had broken into your back door. The blood was his, and the gun they found by his body was the one that killed the guy just off the porch. My guess is as Rocky was spinning the guy by his leg, he was trying to shoot Rocky but ended up shooting his buddy. When he finally got free and ran, he was met by the guy that sent him with a .22. Two to the back of the brain.

"We found a shoeprint that was not either of the two dead men, so the guy in the blue car is out to get you. But why and who was the shooter last night? Because the guy in the blue Chevy had his left hand on the roof of the car, and it looked fine. No hole. The forensic guys said you shot the guy through the left hand. There were bone fragments in the left side of the gun. So they are talking about two people after J.W."

J.W. said, "Great! You're just full of good news."

They finished their meal, got back into the jeep, and started to drive home, keeping an eye on the back trail all the way back. They stopped by the cop shop so Mike could get another car. After that, they went, got gas in the jeep, then went back to J.W.'s place.

They looked at all the tape. The driver's door and the hood had both been opened. J.W. reached in and pulled the hood latch. He opened the hood. There were three sticks of dynamite, a blasting cap with a wire, and a roach clip on the end of the wire. J.W. removed the roach clip from the coil, the other one from the ground side of the coil. He had both clips in his fingers and the dynamite in the other hand. He pulled them out. J.W. removed the blasting cap and made it safe. He looked all over the rest of the car, satisfied it was okay to start.

He and Mike were looking at the dynamite. There was a name there, on the sticks.

"Well, write it down, but don't touch it."

He did.

J.W. put the jeep away. Mike put the dynamite in the safe in the shop and the blasting cap in the ammo locker.

J.W. grabbed the makeup bag and locked everything up. He set the house alarm and said goodbye to Rocky.

Mike was still standing by the car. They got in. They drove out to Miss Ginny's with an eye on their back trail.

They arrived. Richard and two of his men met them.

J.W. got out of the car.

Richard walked over. "Are you okay?"

J.W. said, "Yes, but there's strange things going on around here."

Richard said, "That's why I have the house and grounds around the house in lockdown: to keep her safe."

J.W. said, "Thank you for that. Here's her car back. Have you ever used the Scotch tape trick?"

"No."

"Well," J.W. said, "I did last night, and someone put an IED in the car last night. Check all cars before starting them."

Richard said, "I'll see to it personally."

J.W. shook his hand. He told Mike he will be right back. J.W. went up the stairs to the front door so he could give Miss Ginny her bag back.

As he knocked on the door, a slug hit the door. J.W. hit the deck. Michelle opened the door, and J.W. leaped in, knocking her down, as two more rounds hit the door and the wall inside. J.W. could see Mike and Richard talking; they had no idea what was happening. The shooter had a noise suppressor, also known as a silencer.

J.W. grabbed his phone. He called Mike. He answered. J.W. said, "Sniper."

He dove, taking Richard with him. A round went through the windshield. Richard got on the radio, saying where to look. A few minutes later, there was automatic gunfire coming from two different directions.

They radioed back. "We got him, sir."

Mike and Richard jumped into a golf cart. J.W. was still holding Michelle because when he had knocked her down, she hit her head. She was coming around now.

Miss Ginny got there. J.W. told her to help Michelle. He ran out the side door, just to be safe. He got to where Mike was. There was the body of a man with a wrapped left hand and a sniper's rifle next to him. Mike checked the body for ID; he found none, just car keys.

J.W. said, "This is getting ridiculous."

He looked at the man's face.

"Do you know him?"

"No, he's a merk." *Merk* is short for "mercenary."

J.W. knows his type, big bucks to hire him. Mike bet the other guy was too, but who hired them? That was the question, and why?

Mike said he would handle this.

J.W. said, "I need to get to work."

Richard said he would be driving him and would pick him up later at work. As they left, it looked like half the department was coming up the hill.

J.W. got to work. He showed Richard where he could park and where he would come out.

Richard said okay and drove off.

The night went but slow, so just before J.W. got off work, his friend James let him on the roof so he could watch the area.

The limo pulled in. He could see the dark-blue Chevy pull in across the way. No wonder it looked black earlier. Under the streetlamps it looked black.

That explains a lot.

J.W. called Mike. "Are you there?"

Mike said, "Yes, I'm in the parking lot at the Chinese restaurant."

"Do you see the dark-blue or black Chevy at your three o'clock?"

"Yes."

"That's the guy that was in front of my house."

Mike said, "Okay, I will get the two units I have waiting down the road."

J.W. said, "Okay, Mike. I see them coming."

The Chevy saw them too.

"There he goes." Mike chased the Chevy with the two cruisers, all their lights on.

J.W. went down to the limo. Miss Ginny and Richard were waiting. He rode in the limo. He felt uneasy as they dropped him off at the house. He figured they were tracking his phone.

J.W. had a plan. He checked his phone for spyware. J.W. found it under the cover; it was just a GPS tracker. He had seen a lot of them in his time.

He called his boss. He would not be in tomorrow. He would tell her later why and not to tell anyone at all tonight. He will prepare for tomorrow.

CHAPTER 18

Final Chapter

Wednesday morning

J.W. awoke the next morning to his phone ringing. It was Mike.

He said, "They got the dark-blue Chevy but not the man." He thought J.W. should know.

J.W. thanked him and proceeded with his plan. He got everything set up and loaded last night. He walked out to survey the street. It was about 10:00 a.m. He looked over his suspect's list: there was the ex-boyfriend who wrecked his Ferrari trying to get away from J.W., someone from his past, or Miss Ginny's brother, Mark.

"Haha." J.W. laughed to himself. Miss Ginny and her father were out; wrong temperament. Maybe someone else. They would find out today.

He had Mike come by. J.W. told him his plan.

Mike had the same answer he always had: "Are you nuts? That's the most demented plan I ever heard."

"I knew you would love it!"

J.W. showed him the tracker.

Mike asked, "How did they get this on your phone?"

J.W. said, "I'm not sure. But here's where they are going."

"You *are* nuts."

J.W. handed him a new phone, and J.W. had one also. They put his plan in motion.

J.W. drove the jeep out. Mike locked things up. J.W. drove along I-44 west over the Arkansas River, into West Tulsa to the I-44 and 244 interchanged to the West Fifty-First exit, over to W Forty-First west to Highway 97 to Highway 51; out to Keystone Dam Road.

Under the dam was an off-road area. He drove the jeep way into the back area and parked it just far away enough from any roads. He set up his dummy with the same clothing he had on. Anyone tracking his phone could find him. J.W. then pulled his ghillie suit and rifle and moved to a hilltop not too far away.

He set up in the tall grass. J.W. had a clear view of 180 degrees. He lay there, waiting. He heard someone walking up behind him. J.W. had turned the phone to silent already so no sound could give him away. As the man stood next to where J.W. was lying, he watched the jeep.

J.W. hit the remote on the jeep. It started, and the man crouched down and pulled his rifle up and took a shot at J.W.—well, the J.W. dummy. As the bullet hit, the dummy fell out of the jeep.

At that time, J.W. jumped up from the ground just behind him. J. W pulled his knife. J.W. grabbed the man with his left arm, held the knife to his throat, and pulled him down. The rifle fell a few feet away from him. J.W. turned him over and cuffed him. J.W. picked him up off the ground.

It was the ex-boyfriend.

As J.W. pulled him in front of him, a shot rang out. It hit him right in the chest. The shot went through him and hit J.W. All J.W. could think was, *What the hell?*

He hit the ground with Miss Ginny's ex-boyfriend's body on top of him. J.W. could hear someone walking up. It was Miss Ginny's brother with a .308 rifle. J.W.'s chest felt like it had been hit with a sledgehammer. J.W. could barely move; it hurt so bad.

Miss Ginny's brother pulled the rifle up to shoot J.W. "You dared to touch me and my family? You're not—"

His head exploded, and his body fell sideways.

J.W. tried to move out from the bodies. It hurt so bad. He stood up. Mike was running to him. As he saw J.W. stand, he stopped and got on the phone to get J.W. some help. Mike walked over to the jeep and put the dummy in the back, took the chips from all five mini camcorders and put them in his pocket, and then drove over to where J.W. was sitting on a rock trying to remove the bulletproof vest. It weighed about sixty pounds. It was made for high-powered rounds.

Mike got to him and helped J.W. Mike looked at his chest. "You're going to hurt for a while, J.W."

"Ya, I know," J.W. said. "I didn't say it would be easy."

Mike checked the bodies.

"Are they dead?" J.W. asked.

Mike said, "Ya, they're way dead."

"Well," J.W. said, "I can kiss Miss Ginny goodbye. I just killed her brother."

Her father wouldn't be happy with him either.

The paramedics arrived, checked J.W. out, and gave him something for the pain before he could tell them no, but he admitted he did feel better. They put him on a gurney and put him in the ambulance that took him to St. John's Hospital.

The bullet impact did more damage than he thought. It bruised his heart and broke two ribs, but other than that, J.W. was alive.

Miss Ginny didn't come see him in the hospital for the week J.W. was there, but April, his boss, did. So did his friend from the bar, and his friend Patrick came too.

He said, "The guy from the blue Chevy is no longer a problem." He asked J.W. if they had any beef.

J.W. told him, "Peace has been redeemed, and we are cool." After that, he smiled and became the guy J.W. knew.

He said, "When you're ready, first rounds on me."

J.W. told him he was on. After all the commotion, Mike had a lot of explaining to do. He told just how it happened, and a little man came and handed his boss a form that stated he was working for the state department at the time of all these actions. He was taken and to stop all actions; it was a federal case now, and he was protected.

Mike went to J.W.'s place to take care of Rocky because he was the only guy whom Rocky will let in, and he promised to until J.W. could get home.

Mike was there at J.W.'s place when a cab pulled up. J.W. got out.

He went in to get his wallet J.W. had left at the house. Mike paid the cabby for him. J.W. went in and showered and shaved.

As he got dressed, Mike came in and said, "Thanks for saving me from the department."

J.W. smiled. "I don't know what you're talking about."

Mike just looked at J.W., smiled, and said, "Smart-ass." He punched J.W. in the arm.

J.W. winced.

Mike said, "I'm sorry, I forgot."

J.W. said, "Well, is everything back where it's supposed to be?"

Mike said in a military voice, as he snapped to attention, "Yes, sir. The jeep parked, washed, and fueled. Weapons cleaned and in the vault. Suit clean and in locker. Camcorders back in box. Phone on charger minus tracking device, destroyed, and dog waiting to lick you to death."

J.W. looked. Rocky was sitting, waiting for permission.

J.W. called him over. He was all wiggles again and glad to see him.

J.W. looked at Mike. "It sounds like you deserve an ice-cold beer or ten."

Mike smiled. "Now you're talking." He gave Rocky a treat.

Mike set the alarms.

J.W. said, "On guard, Rocky."

They left.

Mike drove and asked, "Any word from Miss Ginny?"

J.W. said, "Nope, not a word."

They got to the Harvard sports bar. Renee was working. They walked in, and she had their beers and shots at their usual spots at the bar. Ashley and Alyssa were sitting there, bullsh——tting about some guy or something. Amber walked in for shift change. Renee was the first bartender J.W. met when he first came in here.

People came by to say hi and BS a bit.

As they were having their fourth round, Renee said, "Your girl-friend just came in."

J.W. said, "I don't think she's my girlfriend anymore. I killed her brother."

Renee got a surprised look on her face. It was Miss Ginny.

J.W. walked over to her, waiting to be yelled at. He stood in front of her.

She flung her arms around him. "I'm sorry my brother was such a sh——t. Are you okay?"

J.W. said, "I am now."

She looked at him with tears in her eyes. "Can you forgive me?"

J.W. stepped back. "What is there to forgive?"

She hugged him again, so tight J.W. couldn't breathe.

As she finally eased up, J.W. asked her, "What changed your mind?"

"The video Mike left with my father. He made me watch. We both know you had no choice."

"Your father's okay with it too?"

"He thinks it's his fault. He wasn't around much when my brother was growing up. I'm just glad you're okay."

J.W. said, "I still have a hole in my heart."

He got down on one knee there in the bar. The whole bar went quiet. J.W. asked Miss Ginny if she would marry him and fill the hole in his heart.

She just stood there with tears running down her face.

J.W. stood up. "Is that a yes?"

She finally got her voice to say something. She screamed, "Yes!"

The whole bar exploded into cheers. All the bartenders hugged Miss Ginny. They said, "You're getting one hell of a man."

They turned to go. J.W. paid their tab, and she told the girls, "You're right, and I'm keeping him."

With a ring on Miss Ginny's finger, J.W.'s life was about to take a new turn, and he couldn't wait to see what was next.

ABOUT THE AUTHOR

 J.W. Wallace grew up in Santee, California, in 1970–1982, where he joined the army. While in the army, he earned his degree in automotive engineering, which he still uses today.

A few friends told him he should write a book, so he did. He hopes you'll like it.